Letters from the Heart
Patrick R. DiCicco

P&D Publishing—Bakersfield, CA
ISBN: 978-0-692-15097-9
Library of Congress Control Number: (pending)
Letters from the Heart | Patrick R. DiCicco
Available Formats: eBook | Paperback distribution

There's a place in our mind where love grows eternal. To men, it may be compartmentalized in the brain and taken out when necessary, but to women, it may be so strong as to consume their emotions. It can be comparable to a beautiful spring garden, or unfortunately sometimes, to where heartache's flow like a raging river. We have all felt the joy and happiness that love can radiate and the glow that can move mountains. We also have fought the bitter taste of melancholy tears when love has brought us to our knees. This story is mine and perhaps it is yours. It is timeless. It will take you on a rollercoaster ride that has no bounds. Come with me and see how love grows but never dies.

Chapter One

We were flying above the weather now, a stormy day with patches of clearing. There is nothing like having a jet engine between your legs. Talk about a power trip and an E-ticket ride!

Your mind wanders when you're in the sky. We carried enough armament to destroy a small city and were traveling at 600 mph. Other than the roar of the engine, it is silent and peaceful, a calming effect I can't describe as you and your plane are one. You think of a lot of things and your view is infinite, but your mortality is always in full view when you are on a mission. It only takes one mistake to fulfill your destiny. We were flying at 22,000 feet and were prepared to drop to 8,000 feet when the Mu Ghia Pass came into view. We also had to be on the lookout for Mig 21's, as they were much more maneuverable than we were and their kill rate was 9-1 in their favor. Flying in formation, we broke off from each other and swooped down on the Ho Chi Minh Trail below. There were four jets today in our sortie, two airmen per plane, and our F-4 Phantoms were loaded to the max. We got down low enough to be silent to our enemy before we swept over their hill. One after another we strafed the long line of soldiers and supply wagons below with our 20mm. Vulcan cannons and Sidewinder missiles, our Napalm bombs lighting up their caravan like the fourth of July. Flying behind enemy lines wasn't new, but this mission carried more danger than the rest. It was at night, in a monsoon and behind the DMZ, a place off limits to us, courtesy of the United Nations. Knowing the roar of our F-4's might announce our arrival, I was glad it was a stormy, cloud-filled night. Today, a C-130 gunship attacked the area before we arrived. Unfortunately, because of our routine, it also announced our coming.

The moon was obliterated by dark ominous clouds as me and my squadron made our descent through the sky above the mountain-filled jungle. Even on a dark and stormy night, I knew we were in for trouble because our plane's outline would be visible against the dark clouds above us.

Then my instrument panel lit up and an alarm went off. I was locked on by the enemy and immediately tried an evasive maneuver. Then bam, out of nowhere, I got hit by a Surface to Air Missile. SAM's were one of the enemy's most potent defense weapons. I immediately lost hydraulics and saw my rightwing tear apart. I was going into a death spin, completely out of control. My navigator and I had to eject and we had to eject quickly because our altitude was less than 2,000 feet when we got hit. I pushed the button and we were rocketed into the rainy sky, instantly leaving the plane at 3 G's. As our chutes opened and we descended, I saw our plane hit the ground in the distance in a fireball.

Then it started! Bam, bam, bam, the dotted flames of gunshots lit up the jungle floor below like a Christmas tree as our chutes opened and we glided closer to the ground. You could tell the rapid report of an AK-47 by the sound and it didn't sound good when you were the target. So down we went, while the sound and sight of enemy rounds fired around us. There were only four fighters on this mission and we were all in jeopardy. As quickly as I saw the upcoming hill, I was bouncing off palm trees. As I covered my head to protect myself I came to a stop, dangling by my chute 15-20 feet off the ground. I had to act fast. I pulled my knife and cut the cord, falling to the ground. I was thankful the foliage was thick and the ground was soggy, or I could have broken my leg. It was protocol to wrap the chute and bury it, but we were already detected. Screw the chute. Survival was in order now. This mission was in jeopardy now, as we were to begin air attacks on the famous Ho Chi Minh Trail. Now they know we are here and the hunt for us begins.

The Ho Chi Minh Trail was Charlie's main artery for troops and armament. It consisted of a series of paths, roadways, and waterways used by North Vietnam to supply its armies in South Vietnam during the Vietnam War. All of the NVA's (North Vietnamese Army) supplies and most of their troops moved down the Ho Chi Minh trail from North to South Vietnam. The Trail was located mostly in Laos and Cambodia, countries that neighbor Vietnam. Due to political restrictions during the Cold War, the U.S. could not invade Laos or Cambodia to shut the trail down, though we did frequently attack it with air strikes. Our mission today was a prerequisite for a major strike next week.

Our main focus was the Mu Gia Pass. It was the main north entry point of supplies and troops headed for the Ho Chi Minh Trail. The topography below was filled with bomb craters, as B-52s carpet bombed it pretty thoroughly in the past. Our mission today was the first phase of Operation Rolling Thunder, and the first facet of our mission was to find and destroy the underground tunnels in which they traveled. Because of the carpet bombing, tunnels became their main way of moving troops North to South and they had to be detonated.

All of a sudden, it got deathly quiet. In the jungle at night you could hear everything, from palm fronds blowing, weeds being crunched by footsteps, an occasional animal, everything except snakes. Because of the attack on us while we descended, I couldn't use my radio to contact my squad. The signal would alert the VC to our whereabouts, and we knew they were everywhere. We were on their turf now and it wasn't a surprise visit any longer. Then a blast of wind hit me and the sky was filled with a warm heavy mist, gradually turning into gales of windswept water. Another monsoon!

I was crawling now, crawling ever so quietly and carefully. Not only were we subjected to Charlie and their land mines, we were in a snake infested tropical jungle. As I crawled, I sadly came across my navigator who was killed before he landed, his parachute wrapped around him covered in blood. "I'm alone now," I thought. I looked at my friend hanging in the tree, cut his strings and let him fall into my arms. I removed his side arm and the dog tag from his neck, covered him with palm leaves, said a prayer for him and was on my way. I had to get to higher ground before daylight. I figured I had three hours before daybreak and I knew they'd be searching for me when they found my chute. Capturing pilots was number one on their agenda. It was a feather in their cap. They not only tortured them for information and used them for bartering, but they paraded them through the streets for propaganda sake.

The jungle was thick with foliage as I slowly made myself up the mountain. Although my visibility was severely limited and the hillside was heavily covered, my thigh muscles told me when I was going uphill. For some reason, the falling rain relaxed me and made me focus. After what seemed like hours, I got to the top of a hill with a steep-sided cliff in front of me and looked down on the Mu Ghia Pass.

When daybreak hit I saw a large convoy of Charlie traveling south in the fog and smoke-filled valley below. I got on my radio and got in touch with the local airbase near Quang Tri Provence and ordered a sortie approximately one kilometer from my coordinates. I sat and waited, covered now with camouflaged leaves and branches, for the airstrike to begin. Even though it was only dawn, it was hot and humid already. Perspiration dripped off my head as I watched them scurry about. It must have been only 10-15 minutes and a squadron of F-4 Phantoms strafed the area below, dropping an assortment of 500 pound bombs, destroying a large area and creating havoc. An ammunition carrier was also hit, lighting up the area and creating a large mushroom of smoke beneath me. They all scattered like ants. They also knew someone coordinated the attack and would be heading for high ground. Although I knew a rescue chopper would be following, I had to be alert to everything. I was their prey now.

They knew the air attack had to be ordered from higher ground, so this would be one of the first places they would look. While attempting to stay in the jungle and avoid the clearing, I crawled down the mountain slowly, listening to everything and anything as I went.

Then the ground suddenly gave way beneath me and I fell into a hole. I instantly knew my doom, as we were trained for this. As a reflex, I automatically protected my head as I fell and then hit bottom, screaming in pain as I landed. My lower legs were impaled by two punji sticks, one sticking out through my uniform. I was bleeding profusely and tried not to move. I let it bleed a little to clean out the wound and then carefully removed the punji sticks from my leg and cut my shirt with my knife to make a tourniquet. I knew I was in trouble because Charlie usually rubbed the sticks in feces, the reason being if the stick didn't kill you the poison and bacteria would. As I quietly watched and listened I grabbed my pistols and laid on my back. I pointed my .45's skyward towards the daylight above me and waited. I knew I was going to either hear a Huey or I was going to hear Charlie. My fate was out of my hands now.

Chapter Two

It was a bustling steel mill town where it all began, an industrial town made up of a melting pot of European immigrants and blue collar people. We called it a melting pot because every ethnic group lived in their own area; i.e. Greeks, Italians, Polish, Slovaks, Puerto Ricans and Blacks. They all had their own church and ethnic food stores. Our hometown was a suburb of Youngstown, Ohio, a steel producing giant that employed and was responsible for the areas economy. Fear of God and American values were the norm, as grit and determination abounded there. You could say it was middle America. This is where I met Diana.

I reached in my pocket and pulled out the picture of my fiancée and kissed it. Perhaps this would be the last time I saw her, I thought. So I calmly closed my eyes and reflected on the first time I saw her and smiled. It was a peaceful time in my life and distracted me from the harsh reality I found myself in. I was a high school senior laying on the lawn under a tree, conversing with some friends when I first met her. The local high school was a large three-story brick building and very imposing, especially to new students. It was the first day of school and the summer sun was hot. The lawn of the high school was filled with students awaiting the bell, some mulling around, some just sitting on the grass discussing the upcoming year and getting acquainted under the two large Sycamores that framed the building. It was a time when the kids from the melting pot of our steel town came together and met at the only high school in town, some for the first time.

I knew everyone in school, but the girl I was staring at was new. She showed up with two other girls, neither of which looked familiar. She was pretty, perky and petite, her black hair and dark brown eyes were a definite distraction from her pretty smile. She walked with an attitude and carried a confidence that spoke volumes and commanded attention. She stood about ten feet away, talking to her friends and glancing at me every few minutes while she smiled, pretending I wasn't there. I soon found out that shyness wasn't in her DNA either as she looked down on me as she walked by, saying hello as she passed. I nodded while turning my head and watched her enter the building. Notwithstanding, something in me told me I wanted to see her again.

It wouldn't take long. It was twelve o'clock and the smell of the cafeteria filled the school. While standing in line with my tray in hand, she approached me and asked if she could cut in line. "I hope you don't mind, I'm in a hurry," she said. I replied it wasn't a problem as we locked eyes for the first time. "Yeah, right", she said and laughed. She introduced herself and I admired her moxie. While we stood in line we talked a little, but what I remember most is how good she looked and how good she smelled. I couldn't help but check her out as she stood in front of me with her back turned. Then, the next day she did the same thing.

Driving home from school that week, I saw her walking with some friends. I pulled my Chevy over and asked her if she wanted a ride. She blushed and said sure, but her friends would have to come too. No problem for me! We stopped at Isaly's on 12th St. and got a skyscraper cone before I dropped them off one block from her house. She was scared to death her brother or father might see her as I soon found out she was only in 9th grade, which totally shocked me. As well as having a beautiful figure, she looked and carried herself as being much older. This brought with it a whole new set of circumstances. We were going to have to be very careful.

And we were. We saw each other discreetly whenever we could. She would tell her parents she was over her girlfriends house whenever we would go out. Going out was the Bowling Alley on 422 near the state line of Pennsylvania, which was only 5 miles away, Idora Park and Mill Creek Park in Youngstown, or many of the Church Festivals in the area. We loved and laughed and slowly watched love grow.

It was on a cold February night in 62' that I gave her my graduation ring. It was after a birthday party for a friend of mine, his birthday being a week before mine. She stared at it and cried with excitement. We went steady after that, as if we weren't already. She would wear it on a chain around her neck at school and then pocket it when she got home. Heaven forbid her family should see it.

I remembered how we dated my senior year in high school, and how it continued while I went to College. Because of her strict Italian heritage and our age difference, she had to sneak out all the time, even when she was a senior.

Trying to escape the moment, I closed my eyes and recalled the first time we made love;

she was 17 and a junior in high school and I was 21. I guess you could say we put it off as long as we could. It was a beautiful summer day and her parents had gone to the Ice Capades in Cleveland for the day and she invited me over around one for dinner. I knocked on her front screen door and heard her yell to come in. As I walked into the foyer she replied, "I'm upstairs, come on up". As I walked up the staircase, I realized her voice was coming from the bathroom. I walked in to see her sexy body laying in a bubble filled tub smiling and pointing and curling her finger at me, as if she wanted me to come closer. "Do you like what you see," as she enticingly smiled again? That was all it took. I removed my shoes and got into the tub fully clothed, while both of us laughed. I kissed her passionately as she pulled me toward her and undressed me. We made love in that hot water and both reached orgasm at the same time. Afterwards we laid there just hugging and talking while the water got cold. Then she got up and dried off as I watched her. She had a magnificently sculpted body and made me wonder why we waited so long. She kissed me before she walked into the bedroom, grabbing my penis and enticing me to follow. I dried off and found her lying on the bed, her beautifully tanned body complimenting her pink bedspread. We had made love haphazardly in the tub, but this time it was romantic. As she laid there I kissed her on her lips and slowly caressed and kissed her on the nape of her neck, her ears and her beautiful perky breasts. I slowly licked her belly button and made my way slowly to her inner thighs, teasing her now. She squirmed and moaned passionately as my tongue entered her ever so gently. I climbed on the bed and laid there so she could return the favor. She grabbed my penis and teasingly put it in her mouth, licking me all over. After what seemed like an hour, we both exploded at the same time, her beautiful body quivering in my mouth and hands.

Then I closed my eyes and rehashed some more of the good times we had. There were nights bowling at the Lincoln Knolls Bowling Alley with snacks across the street at Gaetano's Airport Tavern. There was dancing at Idora Park on Saturday nights, with pizza and beer at the Elmton on the way home. The Sky-Hi Drive-In in my convertible in the summer was always fun, while picnics at Mill Creek Park on Sundays brought out her cooking skills. We walked together, laughed together and loved together. Every day was a holiday. As the years passed, we both graduated at the same time, she from Campbell Memorial and me from Cal Poly. It was then I then became "acceptable" to her family, mainly because I was of Italian descent like her.

It was 1967 now and Vietnam was cranking up on the horizon. I always wanted to become a pilot and knew I'd be drafted into the Army after graduation. So, because I was a college graduate, I did a pre-emptive strike and enlisted in the Air Force and became an officer. But I couldn't leave for the service like this. Diana and I had talked about getting married many times when I finished college. So I sold my new GTO and bought her an engagement ring before I left. After asking her father for her hand in marriage, we drove up to Niagara Falls so I could propose in a beautiful setting. It was a warm summer night as we sat eating dinner atop the space needle overlooking the Falls. I had given the engagement ring to the Maitre de' when we got there and asked him to put it in the bottom of a glass of Champagne I'd be ordering. As we sat there and talked, I nervously watched as she drank her champagne without seeing the ring. Then it happened. She stopped and stared at the ring and then me. She removed the ring from the glass and looked at me crying with excitement. I then grabbed the ring from her hand and got on my knee in front of everyone and asked her to marry me. She was ecstatic and our last night together was memorable to say the least. We made a date to be married one year from that June night at St. Lucy's Church in Campbell.

I had a few days before I left for Basic Training at Lackland Air Force Base in San Antonio, Texas, and we spent them all together. I left from the Erie Terminal in Youngstown for the physical in Cleveland on a rainy day. Diana cried as she hugged me and kissed me goodbye. I sat at my seat at the window and waved to her as the train slowly departed, not knowing if I'd return and thinking about our wedding in a year.

After eight weeks of Basic Training I was sent to Officer Training School at Maxwell AFB in Alabama for a nine-week intensive course and then to pilot school at the USAF Academy in Colorado. After being trained on a T-33 back at Lackland, I graduated to an F-4 and was to be whisked off to Vietnam after a short leave. The whole process took about a year and change.

Being this might be my last leave for a while, I met her at Niagara Falls and we slept in a Motel with a room overlooking the Falls. It was a wonderful weekend. Our wedding had to be delayed and she understood this, even though it hurt her. We had to change plans and marry once I returned from the war. I simply didn't know my future and didn't want to ruin hers.

In the meantime, she attended college at Youngstown State University to become a teacher. We stayed in touch as much as possible. I saved all her "I love you's" in my foot locker at the base and thought of her always.

Chapter Three

Just then, I heard a noise and came alive again, bringing me back to the moment. The sun created a shadow on the side of the hole I was in, creating an eerie effect with the jungle as a background. My legs were throbbing and beginning to get numb. I knew shock was setting in as I was also getting light headed. All of a sudden, a smoke grenade landed a foot away from me. I reached for it and immediately tried to throw it out, but it hit the top of the hole and came back down on me. I tried to throw it out again, but my hand was burning now and I couldn't see. I coughed and couldn't breathe and soon passed out.

I came to as I was being lifted out of the rabbit hole by four Viet Cong. I was in great pain, but I could breathe again. I was then placed on a bamboo stretcher and tied down. After walking for a while we walked into an underground tunnel for what seemed like hours and hours. We emerged from the ground in an old thatched shack where I was then beaten. As they questioned me, they kept beating me until I lost consciousness again.

When I came to I was hog tied and transported in a truck wearing nothing but a blindfold and my shorts. We traveled for hours before we arrived at a POW camp. I was "interviewed" and beaten again. I refused to talk while they laughed at me and kept beating me until I was unconscious.

When I awoke my legs were bandaged and I was lying on the floor in a dark room with no windows. My face was swollen and caked with black dried blood. I felt nauseated and dizzy and thought I had a concussion. A bowl of rice and a bowl of water was lying on the ground next to me. I could also see the glowing eyes of a couple of rats in the corner, hungry rats, I thought.

"Why are they keeping me alive?" I wondered. "How stupid of me. They got another pilot!"

I tried to drink some water, but my lips and mouth were so swollen I could hardly sip. I closed my eyes and thought of Diana again. It was my escape from this hellhole. The goal of the North Vietnamese was to get written or recorded statements from the prisoners that criticized U.S. conduct of the war and praise how the North Vietnamese treated them. Such POW statements would be viewed as a propaganda victory in the battle to sway world and U.S. domestic opinion against the U.S. war effort. Pilots were treated differently. Not only were we beaten, we were psychologically abused too. We were often marched through the streets of Hanoi with placards around our neck, denouncing the American war effort. Sometimes we were drugged and put in front of a TV camera denouncing America.

Then it got worse. The few of us that wouldn't bend were transferred to the camp they called the Hanoi Hilton. The torture was constant. We were thrown in tiny cells, slabs of urine stained concrete for beds, and single, bare lightbulbs turned on 24x7 making sleep impossible. We were in a constant state of starvation, and when we were fed the watery soup was laced with pebbles or feces. We were made to stand on stacked fecal stools for days on end. We were often strapped down by 15-pound leg irons, which caused lacerations and infection, or locked to wooden stocks at the ends of our beds, which kept us on our backs for days. This not only was painful but standing afterwards was almost an impossibility. The walls and floors were overrun with roaches and rats. When we were strapped down, we were forced to lie in our own excrement, the acidity breaking down our skin.

To keep me sane, I would write letters or stare straight ahead and daydream. According to the Geneva Convention, we were allowed to write a letter once a week. Not here though. We wrote once a month, and they were apparently thrown away because we never got a letter in return. "Diana, where are you? Why don't you respond to my letters," I often wondered? Knowing she'll be notified of my absence will worry her for sure, I thought. As the months turned into a year and then two, she became a distant memory. I knew she had a life and I wasn't in it, not anymore. My love for her made me wish she was happy. I wanted her happy and I didn't expect her to wait any longer. Knowing she was happy brought me solace. She probably thinks I'm dead, I thought. So I wrote her one last letter, not knowing how long I could hold on and not ever knowing if she'd get it.

"Dear Diana,

I just wanted to drop you a line to let you know I'm doing fine, and I don't want you to worry about me anymore. But somehow, though we're apart, I don't feel like I'm away from you. I close my eyes and we're together. I smell you, I feel you, and I taste you. Your presence is that close, yet so far. My hope is I could take your edge off, if only for a minute, as I know how tense you can get. Don't let your feelings of regret, anger, and sadness build a barrier between us, as I have always been here for you and I always will. The situation we're in is part of the rigorous journey we call life and may be a test from above. Only time will tell. I also ask that you don't put the weight of our separation on your shoulders, as we will be together again, somewhere, someway. I promise you, I will love you with all my heart and protect you in all ways possible. It may also be possible I will return at a time when you least expect it, or I may not return at all, for destiny is not in our control. Keep the candle glowing, for the flame that burns in me is more powerful than anyone knows.

Ti amor sempri

Pasquale "

We were at the Hanoi Hilton just short of 2 years, and then 10 of us were sent to a camp near the Ministry of National Defense in Hanoi that other prisoners called Alcatraz. It was probably the most remote of all and was reserved for the "hard core" prisoners, prisoners who were deemed valuable and who remained silent.

The hell continued. Their plan here was to isolate us to maintain control. Each cell was separated by an empty cell to hinder communication between us. They were sweat boxes where the temp would climb to 110 degrees in the daytime, making it too difficult to breath with decaying fecal matter everywhere. At this time I discovered that two fellow airmen from my squadron were shot down with me and were imprisoned here. We soon devised ways of communicating with each other, like blinking to the Morse Code when we would pass each other, for example.

After a year, we were transferred back to the Hanoi Hilton, mainly because the North Vietnamese suddenly didn't want to get caught violating the Geneva Convention. After leaving Alcatraz, some of the men thought they'd be going home within days, weeks, or maybe months. But as time continued to go by, some men died and I became weaker. I became unrecognizable, even to myself. When I would look down on myself, it would remind me of the ghastly pictures I saw of Jewish prisoners at the gas chambers in WWII, all skin and bone.

They opened my door one day to a blinding bright summer sun and escorted me to the "psychological stripping room," as they called it. They tied me to a chair and put a gun to my head. I closed my eyes as I said a silent prayer, thinking my nightmare would soon be over. Then "click"...nothing, "click"...nothing again, and "click" again in slow unison, but I was still here. They all laughed. I put my head down and didn't know what to think. Part of me wanted to die. I was mentally beaten. Then a beautiful woman came in the room wearing a tight, red, short silk dress. I couldn't help but admire her beautiful figure and pretty skin, as it's been years since I saw a woman. She sat on my lap and kissed me while caressing my face. Then she slid her hand down my crotch, grabbing my penis, and kissed me again, her perfume driving me nuts. My emotions were off the charts. I went from the fear of being shot in the head to carnal desire and extreme confusion in two minutes. Then she got up and without speaking motioned her comrades over as she slowly walked away, her tight silk dress defining her beautiful body. I didn't know what to expect and thought this was my last day on earth. Then they held my arm down and injected something into my veins and started to laugh again. I didn't know what to expect, but then a rush came over my head, slamming my brain and almost knocking me out, and my pain went away. Everything went away, and my head slumped to my chest. When I came to I was in my cell. I wasn't in pain any longer. I thought they were being kind at first; at least that's what I wanted to believe. I even looked forward to Hanoi Hilda, as I called her. Every day they gave me a hit and I would slump down in my chair. I would awaken in my cell again, feeling no pain. Eventually, I didn't slump over and remained alert....I needed more....I wanted more.

I soon found there was a method to their madness. I would pace my cell yelling and screaming for more. I would shake and lie on the floor in the fetal position, as sleep was impossible. They would bring me to the room and tie me to the chair again. Thinking I would be getting another shot I would wait patiently, sweating while anticipating every movement. Then the questioning would begin, over and over again. No drugs, just a beating because I didn't cooperate. They wanted me to denounce my country on TV. I closed my eyes, gritted my teeth and thought of my Diana while they beat me. Just as I was getting stronger and less dependent, they would hook me again. The cycle repeated itself all over, each time ending with me unconscious and in a stupor.

Chapter Four

The pangs of love and the loneliness of incarceration are unrelenting at times. They tug at your very soul and create feelings in you that are uncontrollable, both defying logic and common sense.

"Diana, where are you? Do you still love me?"

Concussion's are a bitch. They leave you confused and sometimes incomprehensible. My mind then wondered again, as if I was in a dream.

"Diana, do you hear me," I prayed?

I closed my eyes and was back in Campbell again, if only for a minute it seemed. It was a summer day and she was walking at Roosevelt Park with a small white dog, but she seemed to be walking away from me, walking from the Pavilion and exiting the park. My eyes followed her for the longest time. It was as if I didn't exist anymore. I wanted a smile at least, but she never turned in my direction. Little did I know she was walking out of my life, walking slowly down the street, her head down, as well as mine.

"Diana, where are you going? Diana can you hear me?" "You don't know what I'm going through! You don't know what's on my plate!" I called out to her, but there was no response.

It was as if she was gone, both metaphorically and spiritually. Was this dream a premonition, a byproduct of my many concussions, or was it fact? All these years without communication from her was telling me there was a finality to this, the dream a symbol perhaps of her departure, of her leaving me. I didn't want to believe it but it seemed too real. I sat there and tried to remain a positive person throughout and couldn't fathom her leaving.

I then awoke and started shaking again and vomited the food they gave me. Then I blacked out again and saw Diana standing at the end of a dark shadowed tunnel. The tunnel seemed to grow and oscillate as I walked through it. "Diana!" I called out to her, but she seemed to be further away with each second, with each step I took. Then everything oscillated in a blur and went black.

Days turned into weeks and weeks turned into months, but I was still here, still alive, alive with a pulse, but dead in my mind. You can experience death without dying and I was doing it on a daily basis. Why is it I never got a letter, I wondered? Not a day went by without thinking of my Diana.

But, being a man, I have a tendency to compartmentalize everything into boxes which I store in my brain. My hometown has a box, as well as Diana, my family, my high school, my college, my F-4 Phantom, my imprisonment here, and everything else that is significant to me. The boxes are only opened one at a time and given my full focus, and never are they touching. This keeps my emotions in check and keeps me sane, especially during trials like this.

My pain was sometimes unbearable, but I always managed a smile as I recalled some of my happiest times while we dated. That was one of the boxes that kept me alive. She was a bundle of energy stored in a petite container, bold yet vulnerable, bubbly yet volatile, beautiful yet grounded. She was a dreamer, whereas I was a realist. We complimented each other in every facet of life.

Now here I am, MIA and a POW. This was a living hell I was going through. I was at a camp now they called the Briar Patch, a POW prison located about 33 miles north of Hanoi and they were trying to strip me of my identity on a daily basis. They wanted me to talk and relay information about my squadron and our missions. When they would beat me I would close my eyes, shut off my senses, and open Diana's box. I bled, I hurt, I screamed in pain sometimes, but I always thought of Diana. She was the light at the end of the tunnel, the unreachable star, the full moon behind the clouds, beautiful but hidden. Not knowing when I might die, I wrote her again.

"My Lovely Diana,

I have been moved to another prison but I'm okay, so please don't worry as I am treated fine. Although we are apart, I am there as you are here. The times we shared together, your kiss, your touch, and the way you loved me are all what keeps me alive. Part of me is dead, but the thought of you and your sweet lips that move with the voice I love is the rain that grows on the seed in me that is you. And the thought of you grows more in me each day. You are the light at the end of the tunnel and the sun that rises in this hellhole I live in. You are my joy when the day is filled with pain. I thank God every day for bringing your memory to me, and only wish you joy and happiness, a fantasy to me now as I lay here like a caged lion with bridled passion. Diana, we will meet again after I overcome this chapter in my life I call HELL and peace will be ours. Please don't forget me.

Pasquale"

Then they ramped it up. One day I was brought into another room. When they took the blindfold off, I was in a dark room and staring at a video projector showing American soldiers being shot in the head while tied to Palm trees. Then with their slumped heads bleeding profusely, their penis was cut off and put in their mouth. Some men lost their penis before they got shot. I cringed inside because a revolver and a machete were sitting on the table in front of me and they were smiling at me. Then they put the gun to my head and I said my prayers and closed my eyes. Click, click, click, nothing! They laughed and started beating me again. When they stopped they dragged me to my cell.

Years went by and I was still there. My gaunt body was a shadow of its former self, but I was still alive, alive with my pretty Diana living in my mind. They couldn't take that away from me. "What was she doing now?" I often wondered. "Did she move on?" After all I wouldn't blame her if she did. I've been gone for years and I may never get back home. I was exposed to pain and grief on a daily basis, pain that would have broken most men. The conditions here were brutal and many prisoners contracted and died from Beriberi. Malnutrition, rats and mosquitoes were a way of life here. It was my faith in God and my love for Diana that kept me strong. After a while, I would even smile when they would drag me to the interrogation room. Like what else could they do, kill me? I was ready! One day after a beating I was feeling weak and felt death creeping up on me. Feeling mortal, I wrote another letter, perhaps my last, I thought.

"Diana,

When I'm lying on this cold damp floor with my hand over my eyes trying to gain some sanity from the situation I find myself in, I find my mind drifting and wanting to give up. I feel drained and void of feelings, separated from love ones, from the love of my life and the friends that were always there for me. You are there and I am here. Why me? How did I get here? With my eyes closed I wander back to my hometown, to the places that brought me joy.

Various songs also flow through my mind like a canoe slowly wading through murky water, but George Jones' "He Stopped Loving Her Today" really sticks out in my mind.

He said I'll love you 'til I die.
She told him you'll forget in time.
As the years went slowly by....
She still preyed upon his mind.

He kept her picture on his wall.
Went half crazy now and then.
He still loved her through it all....
Hoping she'd come back again.

They found love letters by his bed.
Dated 1962.
He had underlined in red....
Every single, I love you.

I went to see my friend today.
Ohhh, ...but I didn't see nooo tears.
All dressed up to go away....
First time I'd seen him smile in years.

He stopped loving her today.
They placed a wreath upon his door.
And soon they'll carry him away.......

He stopped loving her today.

Ya' know she came to see him one last time.
Oh, we all wondered if she would.....
And it kept running through my mind...
This time he's over her for good.

Pasquale"

Nothing seemed to matter anymore. Diana, my family, my friends, they're all gone now. After all, no one has ever written me. Do I exist, or is this a mirage painted by my overactive intelligent brain? Did I already die and this is hell I'm occupying? I wonder? Hell can't be worse than this. Diana, where are you? Did I deserve this fate? Is this my Karma for my deeds, or am I paying for my sins from another life I once lived. So much to think about; it's a scary tunnel I entered. A tunnel that is dark and eerie, winding and twisting, a vision here and then darkness that only a funeral could bring. Then a black fog envelops me again. I envision myself at my funeral with a line of people gathering at my coffin. I didn't see Diana there though. Does she even know I died, I wondered? Then all of a sudden she appeared.

Chapter Five

On a cold and rainy day the beatings abruptly stopped, and so did the rice bowl with feces. It suddenly appeared we were deserted. Two days went by without food or water. A soldier two cells down from me died from his wounds and a few men were delirious. I was in withdrawal and shaking badly when a new window opened to my world. Armed American troops and medics came walking down the portal and opened the doors one by one, shooting the locks off. I was so surprised I trembled on the ground and couldn't speak. I was shaking badly and tried to point to the scars on my veins but soon passed out.

When I came to, I was in a Medevac chopper headed for Saigon. I was hooked up to IV tubes and an oxygen mask while being overlooked by a medic as we flew. I couldn't believe what was happening. My eyes bulged with fear as I heard the rumble of the engines and prayed we wouldn't crash or get hit by a SAM from Charlie. It was then I found out the war was over and the Paris Peace Accords were signed on February 12, 1973. 1973? My God, have I been down that long?

They said I died that day on that Huey. My body had given up. I died a slow death but after a few minutes I was resuscitated. I was told I flatlined for almost 3 minutes before I started breathing again. They also said I would have died that day for sure at the Hilton if I hadn't been rescued. I lay there in intensive care in a Saigon Hospital strapped in a bed for two weeks going through withdrawals before I could even call home. When I did, everyone was thrilled I was still alive, everyone but Diana. I couldn't find her. After a couple months I was transferred to a hospital in Texas.

The flight to the states made me apprehensive again. The last time I was in a jet I was shot down. But today there were very attentive people looking out for my well-being and comforting me.

To maintain my sanity again, I used to write letters. I couldn't mail them but it helped me because when I wrote I felt close to her. It was a habit I acquired in Vietnam to stay sane.

"Diana,

I closed my eyes and was with you again. When I do, I can feel your beautiful skin and admire your olive eyes and lovely smile. I don't know when we'll meet again but, nevertheless, I won't ever give up looking for you. You are a precious commodity to me, a young woman now, but still my sweetheart in my mind. You are embedded in my heart like a precious jewel. The memories and time together we shared are unforgettable. God will help me find you, i know it. Diana, I love you and I always will. Pasquale"

After months of rehabilitation, I was medically discharged from the hospital at Lackland Air Force Base in San Antonio. Diana had always been on my mind, even though I tried to move on. It wasn't long after I got home I found out she and her family moved away. The worst part was the neighbor said their daughter got married and the family moved, but no one knew where. I missed her badly and used to sit in my car at night across the street from her house and stare and reminisce; I was obsessed. She was my life and the reason for living when I was imprisoned. Our hometown and my memories were the common thread that kept us together. I relived all of our moments over and over again. My heart was aching as I felt her touch and her sweet, soft lips on mine. In my ravished mind, we walked the Canfield

Fair and the Church Festivals in town all over again. We sat in the Warner theater and the Palace and the State Theaters, holding hands and eating popcorn. We ate steak at the Brown Derby and Colonial House. We shared chicken at the Golden Drumstick, Kielbasa at the Tangiers and Spare-ribs at the Airport Tavern. We loved Isaly's Skyscrapers and Handel's ice cream.

But the Pavilion at Roosevelt Park was the place that stuck out in my mind more than any other, the place of our first kiss. I visited it often while I was there, hoping she would walk across the lawn again with her little dog. The memories flooded me. I needed a fix. I wanted to go back to that place in my mind where pain didn't exist. I needed it now because I remembered all too well how it took my pain away at the Hotel Hilton, but I also remembered the pain and anguish my body went through trying to eradicate the poison in my system. I had to move on. I had to forget her. I just had to. But how, I wondered?

I had a degree in Aeronautical Engineering from Cal Poly and moved far from Campbell to Burbank, California, acquiring a job at Lockheed-Martin at their secret Skunk Works. The Skunk Works was a clandestine operation that worked on top-secret military planes and was located in a hangar on the eastern side of the Burbank Airport. It was funded by the CIA and I had to pass a rigorous background check. I loved my job and felt privileged to work there. In 1976 the Skunk Works began production on a pair of stealth technology demonstrators for the U.S. Air Force named "Have Blue". The work and construction took place in Building 82 at the Burbank Airport. These scaled-down demonstrators, built in only 18 months, were a revolutionary step forward in aviation technology. After a series of successful test flights at the Nevada Test Range at area 51, beginning in 1977, the Air force awarded Skunk Works the contract to build the F-117 stealth fighter on November 1, 1978. In our business, that was known as job security.

Then one day it happened. Walking through the office I was introduced to a beautiful lady while standing at the coffee machine. It was electric! Her name was Phyllis, and we started seeing each other regularly. It was something sorely needed in my lonely life. I still loved Diana, but Diana had become a dream, an unattainable dream. Phyllis was seven years younger than me and a native Californian. She had blond hair and blue eyes and a figure to die for, beautiful breasts and a narrow waist accenting her nicely shaped hips; I was smitten. While we dated, we visited a new tourist sight each weekend. Living in Pasadena, the coast was 45 minutes away, the mountains less than an hour away, and Vegas, San Diego, San Francisco, and Tahoe were all within an ear shot. Our time together was medicine for my soul and we gradually fell in love with each other. We married a year later in Vegas and moved to Porter Ranch, an exclusive development 60 minutes from work but out of the L.A. congestion. Even though we were happily married, my heart always remembered Diana and the good times we had. Her memory haunted me and never left my soul.

A year after we married, Pasquale Jr. was born, and then later on four more kids; Tammy, Trish, Michael, and of course Dina. Phyllis was a stay at home mom and devoted herself to the children and their activities. There was always something going on as all of them were active in sports. It was a happy time in my life. There was nothing as precious as coming home from a stress filled day and watching your kids smile.

The company got larger as I got promoted, and in 1989 Lockheed moved the Skunk Works to Palmdale, California, which was close to

Edwards Air Force Base and China Lake Naval Air Station where we tested some of our projects. I was in charge of one facet of Arms Development and was doing well in my field. Phyllis stayed busy with the kids while I got lost in my work.

Although Phyllis and I enjoyed life with our family, there was always something missing. It was almost as if I was living in a facade, the perfect marriage in the perfect town with the perfect family. The Cleaver family, personified, was what it was. I wore a suit to work everyday and Phyllis was the proverbial California housewife neatly attired with a dress and low cut heels. Money was never an issue and we travelled extensively. Oh, we were the best of friends but the passion I longed for wasn't there; it disappeared when she began driving the kids everywhere. It seemed she was never home.

Fun times was watching Pasquale Jr. play football. He was a good quarterback in high school and went on to play for my Alma Mater, Cal Poly, once playing Ohio State in the Horseshoe. We all went back there for that game, meeting my mom and dad who drove down from Campbell. Time went by fast and the kids eventually graduated from college and moved out on their own. It was then I discovered the loneliness in our marriage and it smacked me in the face. All along I had gotten lost in my work and had the comfort of the kids at home. Phyllis and I had been together almost 40 years but now I wanted a divorce. I discovered we had grown separately and had gone off in two different directions. I then became a shell of my former self and got lost in my work again. The world became my outlet, as Lockheed sent me everywhere as a spokesman for military hardware they produced. I must have seen 30 countries in 2 years. It was a good diversion for the loneliness I felt at home. The divorce was mutual with no hard feelings either way, but would take a while because of the property involved.

Because of the turmoil and loneliness involved, I started to seriously think of Diana again. On a business trip to Italy, I was arriving at a train station in Milan when I saw the back of an Italian woman walking away as we slowed down at the depot. I thought I was having a Dr. Zhivago moment as my heart raced with excitement watching her, while thinking of Diana. It of course wasn't her, but she got me to thinking seriously about Diana again, thinking with an obsession that was uncontrollable. In fact, it was at this time I became possessed with the idea of finding her.

The internet was invented and computers not only made my job easier, it became a tool for social interaction, replacing telephones and typewriters, letters and oral and video communication. Because of these new search tools, I got curious and thought it would be easier to find her. I had scanned dating sites to appease my carnal desires but I found as we get older we get set in our ways and our standards are set in concrete. Unfortunately, because of our profound standards, we also shut people out before we get to know them.

At work one day, today's date popped up on my computer and I realized it was Diana's birthday, a date in May I had never forgotten. It was a **Déjà vu** moment that was filled with memories. So I searched her name, her maiden name, and after striking out many times I found her alive and living in Lake Tahoe, Nevada. Lake Tahoe, coincidentally, was my favorite place in the whole world and was only a 6-7 hour trip from my home in California. After finding where she lived, I kicked around the thought of visiting her for months. I was consumed with guilty because I was still married, as our divorce wasn't finalized and I was still at home. I thought about calling her but finally decided to visit her one weekend. So in December I headed for Incline Village, Nevada. Compulsively, or maybe foolishly, I figured I'd surprise her, because I had never contacted her.

Chapter Six

Lake Tahoe is one of the biggest alpine lakes in the world, divided by the boundaries of Nevada and California. It is so deep it's sheer volume could cover the huge state of California in 9 inches of water. Tahoe held many memories for me, both good and bad, but mostly good. I've had a Timeshare there for 38 years, and it was just last year I cycled around the lake, the 72 miles taking me 10 hours. I even got clipped by a car and was sent flying into gravel on the side of the road, the fall to the ground cracking my helmet. But being lucky and highly motivated, I kept on until I finished, eventually arriving at the hotel that night with bloody knees and elbows. To think Diana was that close all these years made me nauseous.

It was a week before Christmas and the snow was blowing hard and beginning to accumulate as I drove around the lake to Incline Village. It was a winter storm and it wasn't unusual for Tahoe to get two or more feet at a time. I once was here for Christmas years ago when 4 feet fell overnight at lake level, with 10 feet falling in the mountain passes, making that Christmas very memorable to say the least. Highway 28 was one of the most scenic roads in America, winding 72 miles around the lake at an elevation that varied from 6200 to 8500 feet. The lake was a beautiful cobalt blue with the white mountains in the background and the falling snow contrasting it nicely, but my mindset was different today; I wasn't admiring the view. Today, nothing was going to keep me from my destination.

It was twilight as I drove into Incline Village, around five o'clock. Christmas lights adorned the estates when I saw the Hyatt Hotel and Casino lit up in the distance. As I looked at the view of the lake, I knew I was finally here. Incline was a small and exclusive resort city on Nevada's north side of the lake with very high property values, the place to live if you made it. A small bungalow near the lake would sell for $1.5 mil, and the estates on the lake in Incline Village, where Diana's address was, varied from $10 mil and went skywards. The wedding scene from The Godfather was filmed on the California side of the lake as well as Fredo's famous "fishing" scene. The TV show Bonanza was also filmed here at a Ranch in Incline Village. You could pay to visit the Cartwright Ranch during the summer months only. It was a beautiful spot she chose to live. Mark Twain once ran the newspaper in the nearby mining town of Virginia City a hundred and fifty years ago, when the Comstock Lode was discovered, and called the Tahoe region the "Jewel by The Lake."

Fifty-four years had gone by since I first met her, and it was fifty years since I saw her last. My mind was running through hoops thinking about the time that transpired. Does she know I'm alive? Is she okay? Is she married? Is she healthy? Will we recognize each other? And most importantly, will she still feel as I do once we meet? My obsession and the questions going through my mind turned my stomach into a mess.

I had her address and drove by her house on the way, but I didn't have her phone number. First of all I had to stop at my Time-share to check in. The Time-share held so many memories for me. It happened years ago but I could still see my two year old son sitting in a high chair with his Pittsburgh Steeler uniform on covered in spaghetti, as well as the floor around him. Then there was the time Pasquale and I came up here by ourselves one year when he was seven and went to Reno to buy him a

Schwinn Scooter. I stood on the balcony that cold afternoon and watched him play with that thing in the parking lot down below for hours. Then there was the time I won a pool tournament here at the Sahara Casino and the time we took the kids skiing at Squaw Valley with my youngest daughter almost crashing into a storage shed at the bottom of a slope....scaring me to death! There were many hiking trips too, both in the snow and summer heat. Those memories are what they are now, memories.

I turned on the thermostat to warm the Condo and walked over to the back sliding glass door and stared at the lake. I'm here and the time has come. Did I do the right thing? Should I have written her first? I was full of anticipation and was compelled to write her another letter. On the Time-share stationary I wrote;

"Diana,

Where do I begin? Do I start where we met on the lawn at Campbell Memorial, or the day of our first kiss at Roosevelt Park? Do we recount the fun we had at our graduation's or our beautiful engagement at Niagara Falls? There were so many memories of what was, and so much hope for what could have been. We did so much in the short time we were together. So much time has transpired but my love for you has never died. It has boiled in me like steam waiting to explode. Will I still love you after we meet? Will I be what you expect? Will you be the girl of my dreams? God help me, but I do love you Diana!

 Pasquale"

When I finished, I put the letter in my pocket, gathered my coat, and drove the mile down to the Hyatt Casino for some liquid courage. I parked under some tall pines, as the Valet Parking was closed. I was pensive. I couldn't believe she was only a half-mile away. I walked in and saw an empty seat at the bar in the Sports Book and approached it. The casino was humming with tourists and convention patrons, with music playing in the background. I ordered a Scotch-rocks and stared at the football game on the big screen. Ohio State was pummeling Indiana, and I reflected on the last game we attended at the Horseshoe together. It was Thanksgiving weekend in 1966, and we met there for the game while we both were seniors, she in high school and me in college. I was home for the holiday and me and Diana drove down from Campbell. It was her first excursion out of town and I let her drive. What a wonderful weekend we had! The weather was a perfect autumn day; "Indian Summer" was what we called it. Little did I know what was coming in the clouds ahead.

Chapter Seven

I closed my eyes for a second, then cupped my glass in my hands, staring at it. I swirled it around, watching the golden liquid glow with the neon sign I faced. I knew this trip would be a complete surprise to her because I never contacted her. I wanted to surprise her, but now I felt I was wrong. Hell, I'm 72 already! Who will want me, I thought? I don't even recognize the man in the mirror anymore. So many questions ran through my mind. Am I interfering in her life? What if she is happily married? She must be married, she lives in a multi-million dollar neighborhood. After all, I am probably dead in her mind. She's had a life and I pray to God it was better than mine. For years, I fought the PTSD Syndrome and would awake at night screaming and sweating profusely. My subconscious mind was scarred deeply with pain and loneliness. Overtly, I was strong and hid it. Covertly, in my darkest hours, it would raise its ugly head like a lion in a cage, always pacing, always wanting out. If only it were that easy! Sometimes it would suffocate me, almost leaving me immobile. But, I told myself that was in the past, a past I've had to confront and conquer. "How will she see me?" I thought. Will my weakness come through or will I be able to smile and pretend it was just a bad dream? I was good at internalizing. I knew I could pull it off. My mind was a roller coaster.

As I watched the game, an attractively petite lady with black hair sat down beside me and put some money into the video poker machine and started to watch the game. When she took off her coat I noticed she wasn't wearing a wedding ring. We made small talk while we both played poker, as the sound of the football game filled the area.

As we talked her cell phone rang. She turned her head and spoke quietly, almost in a hush tone and walked away talking. Being I just met her, I didn't find the call unusual, but couldn't help but wonder what was so personal. After a few minutes she returned and lit a cigarette.

"I love the Buckeyes," I said, looking at the screen and trying to make conversation. "I've followed them for years," as I turned to look at her and smiled.

She seemed to ignore my comment and continued playing video poker as though she had something on her mind, never turning her head. Then her phone rang and she walked away to talk again. When she returned I turned to her.

"Do you come here often?" I asked, feeling stupid.

"I do," she said while looking at her Poker screen. "I live near here, and it's convenient for my gambling habit when I'm bored. Besides, the food is good and it's inexpensive. South Shore and Reno are where the action is but they're almost an hour away. I go there sometimes, mostly for business or shopping, but usually stay close to home. The weather in the mountains can change rapidly."

"Yes, I know the area well. I've had a Time-share in Incline for 38 years now," I said.

"Oh really? What a coincidence," she replied. "You're visiting your Time-share now?"

"Yes, but I have to ask you, are you from Ohio too?" "I kind of detect a dialect from Ohio or Western Pennsylvania in your voice."

"Yeah, right," she said, as she stared at her screen. "I know what you mean. I'm actually from Campbell, a small town on the outskirts of Youngstown," her voice and remark sounding a little familiar.

"Wow, I'm from Campbell too," I replied, as a familiarity came over her. "A long, long time ago, far, far away in another galaxy," I laughed. "Wow, what a coincidence! Two people from Campbell sitting in a casino during a snow storm in Lake Tahoe watching an Ohio State game. What's the odds?"

"Yeah, right!"

"Yeah, right." "That's so funny! That's what my girlfriend used to say all the time," I said. I then anxiously turned to look at her, studying the profile of her face now. "Where in Campbell?" I asked, my curiosity reaching a crescendo now.

"I lived on Eight Street before I moved out of town in early 73'."

Oh, my God! This was happening too quick, I thought. Everything in my DNA was telling me......

"Oh, my God! Diana? Is this really you?" Have I been coming to this town for 38 years and you lived here?"

"Diana?" "How did you know my name?" She turned and looked at me, studying me, now looking intently into my eyes.

"Pasquale, oh my God!" she screamed as she recognized me. "I recognize your eyes! I

thought you were dead! Oh my God, my God!"
She screamed "My God" again as she put her
head in her hands and started trembling.

I had to catch her as she almost fainted. I
reached over and hugged her as she sobbed. I
was welling up and became flooded with
emotions as I held her. She pulled away from
me and looked at me and started sobbing again.
My heart was racing now. After all these years
the woman of my dreams was in my arms and I
was speechless. Years of emotions were piling
up and flooding my brain. So much time had
gone by, and holding her now brought back
thoughts of holding her the night before I went
to the service. I hugged her tightly and kissed
her forehead, smelling her sweet perfume. Tears
streamed down her face as she sobbed and
shook all over.

"Oh God, help me, I feel like I'm going to
faint. Pasquale, where were you? How come
you never answered my letters? What are you
doing here? Why, why, why?"

"My God, Diana, where do I start? So much
has transpired. A lifetime has passed, yours and
mine both. One thing for sure, I never received a
letter from you. You mean you never got one
either?"

"Not one letter, Pasquale, not one!"

"My God, My God, neither did I!"

We continued to hug with neither one of us wanting to let go. I wanted to cry, but years of imprisonment and abuse left me void of that emotion. But my teared up eyes spoke volumes.

"No, I never received one", she said as she hugged me and trembled. "Your folks got a letter from the Department of Defense stating you were shot down and missing in action. We never heard another word, never, and we never received a letter from you. After a few years, I gave up. I thought you were dead Pasquale, I thought you were dead," she said as she hid her face again, crying aloud. "I had to get on with my life! My God, there's so much I have to tell you."

"Come with me Diana, we have to walk and talk. My God, there's so much to talk about. I don't believe what's happening here.

"Have you had dinner?"

"Oh Pasquale! Do you expect me to eat now? After this?"

"I know it's not Campbell out there, but it is snowing. We always loved the snow. Do you want to go for a walk?"

"Oh Pasquale," as she laughed with tears in her eyes. "You're right. This isn't Campbell, and we're in the Sierra's now. You haven't seen winter until you've experienced a storm in the mountains. She smiled again and held both my hands while she gazed into my eyes. Why don't we go to my place and talk? I'll make you some hot chocolate the way you liked it, but we'll have to stop at Raley's first. It's a grocery store up the street. Oh, I want to bite you so hard Pasquale," she said as she smiled.

"Diana, I know the area well. I've been coming here for years, remember?"

"Oh, my God! I forgot!" She said, as we hugged again.

"Yes, my Time-share is on Northwood. Club Tahoe is only two blocks from Raley's."

"I know Club Tahoe too; it's a beautiful place. Oh Pasquale, we've been so close and yet so far," she said, as she started to cry again, her tears tearing at my heart.

As we got in the car at the Valet station, she took a right towards the lake instead of Raley's. There was a glimpse in the clouds as the moon glittered in the lake below us.

"Pasquale, let's go down to the lake. It's cold, I know, but it is so beautiful. I often fantasized about meeting you there. It is so tranquil; there is a park right on the lake. I have so much to tell you!"

I knew of the park, but just remained silent and watched her as she drove, admiring her face, her body, her voice. I was surprised and happy that she fantasized about me too. She rambled on while I just stared at her while she drove in disbelief. After all these years we've finally reunited. I felt like a homing pigeon who found his way after being lost for years. Then she pulled into the park and we stepped out into the snow and walked the short distance to the lake. The wind and snow was blowing hard off the lake when she turned to me and kissed me passionately. She melted in my arms as I felt her tight body shake with desire. The kiss took me by surprise and quite frankly startled me. As she was passionate, I was tense. I wish the kiss would have been on my terms; we both would have enjoyed it more. We kissed for what seemed like minutes and then held hands and stared at the moon's reflection peeking through the storm clouds on the lake.

"Pasquale, I can't tell you how many times I've stood in this spot and thought of you. Do you know I still have a box at home with clippings of you when you played baseball and football. I also have over a hundred letters I wrote to you after I left Ohio that I never mailed. You were always on my mind and I still felt love for you,

even though I thought you were dead at the
time. It was therapy for me Pasquale. Oh, hold
me again. I want to bite you so bad! I can't
believe you're here."

Chapter Eight

We left the lake and drove the short distance to Raley's, where we picked up some Hot Chocolate mix and Bailey's. Walking through the grocery store with her was surreal, as I had been there many times. To think we were together in such a familiar place made me wonder if we had been there together without knowing it.

The snow was accumulating as we pulled into her driveway. She pushed a button and the garage door opened, letting us inside. As the garage door closed, I reached over and held her softly and kissed her gently on her lips, my eyes searching her dimly lit face, trying to revive the past. We kissed passionately again and I felt alive for the first time in years, her tight body melting in my arms. I held her by her neck and gazed into her brown eyes and admired her facial features as the garage light went off. We sat there in the dark, speechless at first, our hands caressing and hugging each other, both seemingly starving for love. As I clenched my chest, she spoke.

"I guess we better go inside, it's getting hot in here", she said, as she fixed her hair and laughed at the fogged up windows.

When we got out of the car we held hands and kissed again at the door before we walked into the house. I tried to hide the pain in my chest I was feeling and put it off to stress. As we entered the foyer, the lights went on automatically, illuminating it softly. Her house was beautiful, a western, mountain motif, constructed of heavy timber beams, cedar walls and a rock wall which held a huge fireplace. As I looked around I noticed a huge Buffalo head on the cedar wall and a Bear rug on the dark wooden floor, which sunk my stomach immediately....a man's presence is what I felt. The decor was too masculine for such a pretty, refined lady. The more I looked around the weaker I got.

"Is she married?" I thought. "Or is she a widow?" We never had a chance to discuss our past. After all, she's living in a mansion!

"Pasquale, would you like that hot chocolate, or would you rather have a drink? I need a drink after all of this."

After seeing the masculine setting I stood in, I replied; "You know Diana, I think I'd rather have a drink instead. What are you drinking?"

"I was going to make myself a Martini; I think I need one now. And you?"

"A Rum Martini with lime would be nice, just a touch of Vermouth....and no ice. I want to feel it."

"Yeah, right," she said!

She laughed as she walked away and entered the Bar area, my eyes admiring her well toned body. The girl I fell in love with all those years ago was in front of me now. I walked around the Great Room as she made the drinks, perusing each and every knick-knack as I tried to talk myself out of my sudden depressed mood. After all these years, here I stand, confronted with pictures, memories that don't belong to me, smiling faces, tell-tale signs of a life i wished I was part of. Why has life been so cruel to me?

"Am I to find out she's married? Has she any children," I wondered?

My stomach churned with the fear of rejection as I noticed a picture on the mantle of Diana and another man hugging in front of a Venice Canal. Oddly, in the corner was a Secretary Desk with a computer and an open album with photos of young women in different poses. Just as I was about to speak, she entered the room carrying two Martini's and sat on the couch. I stood there for a minute admiring this beautiful woman in front of me.

"Where have the years gone?" I said, as I sadly looked into her eyes.

"Come join me Pasquale," she said with a smile, "There's something I have to tell you." I sat down next to her as she handed me my glass, with both of us raising them to a toast.

Glancing at the photo's on the mantel, she raised her glass and said "May our best of yesterdays be our worst of tomorrows." After a couple sips we both looked tentatively Into each other's eyes.

"Who will speak first...," I thought?

Then her cell phone rang again and she excused herself from the room while she talked. After a couple of minutes she returned.

"Pasquale," she says, "I am not sure how to begin, I feel I have so much to tell you. There's so much I have to say."

I stared at her, wondering about her phone calls and being afraid of and not wanting her to unveil a life that I cannot be a part of. I nervously grabbed her hand trying to extend the moment of innocence just a little longer....the fear of the unknown overcoming me.

"Diana, we've been apart for so long, so much water has gone under the bridge. We each have weaved our own intricate web, but somehow a piece of that silk web has brought us together again. Where do we start?"

Seeing she was tentative, I began. I told her of my years of imprisonment and the letters and poem's I wrote to her, almost on a daily basis. I told her how the mere thought of her kept me alive those years. As I spoke, she hugged me tightly and cried again. I got tears in my eyes too as I told her how I looked for her later and when not being able to find her I moved away, far away, to forget the sights, sounds and smells of that steel town and the neighborhood we grew up and fell in love in. I told her of my time in California and how I met my wife Phyllis. I shared it all with her, the good times and the bad. The more she questioned me, the more comfortable I felt and the more I divulged.

After another Martini I confessed to her of the PTSD I had when I returned from my years of imprisonment and torture and how it still affects me. I told her how difficult it was for me to forget the hell hole I lived through. "It was so surreal Diana; one month I was imprisoned and the next month I was making pancakes for a lady friend. One month I was eating soup with feces in it and the next month I was shopping at a grocery store for New York Steaks. I couldn't forget Vietnam. I used to wake up screaming in the middle of the night, scaring everyone in the house. My wife Phyllis tried her best to understand me, but I know it took its toll on her. I think it took a toll on my kids too".

Diana held my hand and looked me in my eyes as I talked, comforting me in a strange way, as if she understood. I told her of my five kids, two of which live in Paso Robles, Ca., one in Tehachapi, Ca., one in Huntington Beach, Ca., and one in San Antonio, Texas, all of which are doing very well. I lovingly described my six grandchildren and how they mean the world to me. She looked at me quizzically as I told her of my family and the divorce I was going through.

"Pasquale, your face lights up when you speak of your kids and grandkids. How could you leave them? Why a divorce at this time of your life?"

"It was a very trying time in my marriage Diana. I wasn't happy, I didn't even look forward to going home from work. My stomach would go into a knot when I approached the house. Everything seemed to be wrong. My wife had put on weight too and always looked miserable to me.

I believed she didn't love me. I convinced myself she never cared about me or my needs and wants and wishes. I started to believe that all I was was a paycheck. Every time she spoke to me, she was nagging and whining. We argued and fought repeatedly because we felt unheard by each other. She also felt betrayed when I told her I was trying to locate you. After that we couldn't communicate at all."

"I'm so sorry to see you in such pain. You don't deserve this."

Then she stood up, took a sip of her Martini and walked to the fireplace and turned around to look at me. She was wearing tight black pants and heels with a black sweater, both defining her body very well. She looked twenty years younger. I grew intensely nervous as she begun to speak, not knowing what may come.

"Pasquale, you've shared your life with me and I understand so much more now, so much more. I'm so sorry I didn't wait for you but I honestly thought you were dead, your parents did too." Then she put her head in her hand; "Pasquale, I'm married. I don't know any other way to tell you."

She looked up at me, her eyes searching my face, her hand holding her drink trembling. I got up from the couch and walked over to her, holding her in my arms.

"I loved you. I've always loved you Pasquale. I am so confused. Please hold me," she asked?

I held her close, her soft, well defined body embracing me, her perfume arousing and mesmerizing me. I put my hand around the back of her neck and stroked her hair as I pulled her head back to kiss her. She met me with a warmness I hadn't felt in years. Her lips brought me back in time to our youth, a time when we were free of the stress of today. We kissed, we touched each other and we felt young again. I picked her up gently and laid her on the couch, stroking her hair back from her face. I kissed her and started to unbutton her blouse when she softly grabbed my hand and stopped me.

"Pasquale, give me a minute, okay? I'll be right back."

As she left the room, the tightness in my chest returned. "What did I say?" "Did I do something wrong? Did I act too fast?" I took some deep breaths and sipped on my Martini and reflected on our youth once again. I walked over to the window and watched the swirling snow falling against the street light. It reminded me of walking Diana home, going down 12th Street at night in a snow storm, so cold and stormy, and yet so beautifully serene.

After what seemed like thirty minutes, she entered the room in a red silk robe, red nylons and heels, smiling at me with her black hair beautifully hanging on her shoulders. I was mesmerized as she spoke, my eyes surveying every inch of her.

"Is this better Pasquale?"

"Wow, what a surprise! You look beautiful!"

She then strolled over to the fireplace bending over to light it, her well shaped ass partially exposed. After lighting the fire she turned around and looked at me mischievously.

"I want you Pasquale, I want you before you leave again," she said, as she walked up to me and gently kissed me, her moist tongue entering my mouth. The touch of her soft body under the silk and the smell of her perfume on the nape of her neck made me feel like I was in heaven. Then she softly pulled away from me.

"Do you remember this," she asked, as she held out her hand with my graduation ring in it?

I stared down at it in disbelief and put it on my pinky, as it didn't fit my ring finger anymore. I looked into her smiling eyes, my eyes getting watery. The sight of it flooded me with emotions.

"My God, you still have that thing?"

"Of course I do, what did you expect? I also have our engagement ring. You were my life once Pasquale."

"And you mine, babydoll."

"Come with me Pasquale."

She grabbed my belt and turned around, pulling me as she walked over to the couch, with both of us sitting down.

She crossed her legs and smiled, "Do you need your drink refreshed Pasquale?"

I laughed...."Not right now Diana. If I did i'd pour it all over you and lick it off," as I turned and gently pulled her to me. As we kissed she grabbed the back of my neck and pulled me down on her. Then she unbuttoned my shirt and grabbed my belt in her hands, undoing it. I gently rolled her over on her side and caressed her body under the silk robe she had on, enjoying her well defined breasts, her nipples getting erect to my touch. I slowly ran my hand down her belly to her sweet spot, which was dripping with excitement. I inserted one finger and then two, massaging her gently. She tightened up when I bent my fingers and touched her g-spot and started to tremble. She grabbed my wrist hard and penetrated my fingers even further. Her head fell back and she arched her back and screamed. I held her close for a couple of minutes while we kissed. The she slowly undressed me, teasing me as she went. She then pushed me on my back and mounted me, swaying her hips in a beautiful dance of love. Time passed in slow motion. Every kiss, every soft touch, we enjoyed as we eventually exploded together in a passionate outburst. Then we laughed as we rolled and frolicked, knowing we were kids the last time this happened.

"Do you remember the first time we made love Pasquale?"

"How could I forget? Every time I look at a bathtub I think of that. My God, what a nice memory!"

"Yes, and on my bed afterwards was the first time we had oral sex. I've fantasized about it since."

"Me too. I've thought about it too. Is that a hint? Come here beautiful, let's see if we still got it."

While lying on the Bear rug, I reached over and place her on top of me, with both of us kissing each others inner thighs. She was wonderfully sexy the way she enveloped me in her mouth, her warm and wet tongue driving me crazy. I know I hit home too as I felt her tremble again. We then rolled on our sides as she moaned in ecstasy, and I yelled out in a pleasure-pain yell as she consumed me draining me of my fluids. We then cuddled into a hugging position and stared at the fireplace, it's embers a golden orange now.

"I haven't felt so alive in years Pasquale. I still don't know if this is really happening or if I'm dreaming? It all happened so fast."

Chapter Nine

We laid there holding each other, both wanting to speak, but not wanting to ruin the moment. Diana had told me she was married, but the last half hour confused me greatly. I could see she still loved me, and I could sense the confusion in her eyes. But her body and her touch spoke volumes. I had questions, but I didn't know if this was my fire to poke around in.

"Pasquale, you probably think I'm terrible. I told you I was married and now this!"

"To say it didn't confuse me is an understatement. Let's just say I'm glad we shared our passion, but honestly, I am confused. Where is your husband? You never did say."

"Pasquale, my husband is a retired CIA Operative. He caught a bullet a few years ago in Afghanistan on a secret mission to overthrow the Government there. He has debilitated to a vegetable state and lives in a VA Hospital in Bethesda, Maryland. I can't help him any longer, no one can. This is my life now. I live here alone and wait for the damn phone to ring."

Diana cried and sank her head into her hands as she spoke. I reached over and held her to me, not knowing what to say, her half naked body confusing the issue.

"it's a deJa vu moment all over again. I wait for a phone call from him like I waited for a letter from you. I feel like my whole life has been in waiting for death to come."

I held her close and stroked her hair while she continued.

"Pete and I met at a dance at Idora Park after I graduated from Youngstown State. You had been missing almost four years then, and like I said, we all thought you were dead. He was originally from the Southside and went to Woodrow Wilson, and then Stanford in California. He was home on vacation from his job in Washington when we met. He is eleven years older than me. We dated for about a year, with him coming home every chance he got, and then married and moved to Virginia, outside of the D.C. area. I taught school there for years while he came and went on his government missions. We moved to the Tahoe area about twenty years ago and I taught here in town at Nevada College. It gave me peace of mind while he was gone so much. You see, I never knew when he wouldn't return....just like you. That fear has haunted me every minute of our marriage, almost every moment of my adult life, the fear of the unknown. There's so much I have to tell you. There's so much more to my life. Everything isn't what it seems."

Being caught in the moment, I spoke incoherently, not wanting to talk about her husband.

"Wow, I've been coming here once or twice a year for 38 years and never saw you. I can't believe this. I don't know what to say. Damn, so many years have passed."

"Yes, so many years have passed; you probably saw me once or twice and didn't recognize me. How could you know I was here then?"

I then clenched my chest again. The strain and stress of the moment was overpowering. All I could think of again was the sad analogy of Dr. Zhivago being taken from his lovely Lara in the Russian Revolution as a young man and then searching for her his whole life. Then the sight of an aged Dr Zhivago appeared with him riding a bus years later in Moscow and catching a glimpse of Lara walking down a busy sidewalk. How his heart pounded with excitement as he got out and chased her, never catching her and then sadly dying from a heart attack just feet from her as she walked away, with her never knowing it was him. Would this happen to me, I wondered?

"Pasquale, are you okay? What are you thinking? You look so far away."

"I don't know Diana. I feel a tightness that won't go away. Do you have any aspirin? I stupidly left my bottle of Nitro in my suitcase."

"I'll get you some aspirin, but if this is unusual I could take you to the Hospital. We have a small one not far from here."

"Unusual? The whole damn day is unusual. I don't know what to make of it. I don't know where I am or if this is real. Just get me some aspirin please. I got this."

Before she could return I passed out and fell to the floor. I saw her scream and I heard the paramedics arrive and watched from above as they tried to resuscitate me. I was unconscious and probably dead, but I saw it all. I watched her as she cried in the ambulance while they took me to the hospital. On the way there, I entered my body once again. I heard everything, the frantic attempts by the paramedics, the praying from Diana, the siren as we sped down the snowy road. When we arrived at the hospital they placed me in the

Emergency Room where I was attended to by the best that Incline Village had to offer.

Not long after we arrived I left my body again and was talking to someone as we looked down on my lifeless body on the cot.

"Look at you," he said. "Your life is over now, it is time to go. After searching for Diana your whole life, you had the opportunity to meet her and find out for yourself that she is okay. You have been blessed. Now it is time to go

"I don't want to die. Please let me live. There is so much to live for now. Please?"

"You don't understand. Your time is done here. Your many prayers of the past to find her were answered. You were a good man but your carnal life is over. It is time to begin the eternal life your soul has earned."

"No, you don't understand! I'd like to live the rest of my years with her, to make up for the years we missed, to know the Diana that grew in my dreams, to smell her, to taste her, to take care of her. I know she's tempestuous and set in her ways, but I truly love her. She is the soul mate I had to leave behind. Don't let me leave her again. It would be a cruel hand of fate, not only for me but for her too."

Time then elapsed in a darkness I can't explain. It went on and on in a black vacuum without a sense of time or pain; there was nothing. My conversation had ended and a black void filled my being. Then all of a sudden I visited my kids, all at the same time it seemed. Although I will miss them, I watched them in their lives and felt content they were doing well. I walked Roosevelt Park where Diana and I first kissed and stood on the lawn at the high school we met. I travelled the streets of the Steel Valley reminiscing my youth. I relived all of this. Then it got dark and void again. There was no tunnel with a light at the end of it, no noise, nothing. I was torn between heaven and hell as my soul fought for its freedom.

Chapter Ten

Then as quickly as I left my body, I returned to it again. I opened my eyes and turned my head to see Diana sleeping in a chair opposite my bed.

I had an IV and was hooked up to monitors with Oxygen being pumped into my airways. Was I alive? Is this still a dream? I lay there and watched her sleep. How beautiful she was, I thought! Did God allow me to live? Though it seemed real, I couldn't help but think this was a dream.

Then Diana opened her eyes and looked at me. She smiled and walked over and held my hand. A tear rolled down her cheek as she held my hand tightly and kissed it.

"Oh Pasquale, you were out for seven days; we thought we had lost you a couple of times. When you were first hospitalized, they asked me if I wanted your belongings. I took them and found the letter you wrote that day. It was beautiful; thank you."

I tried to speak but I was weak. I felt joy and pain at the same time while I squeezed her hand.

"I love you Diana. There is so much to tell you."

"Just relax Pasquale. You have to relax. You went through a lot. You had a quadruple by-pass and you're lucky to be alive. The Doctor said they lost you twice on the operating table. Why you're still here is a mystery to him. Please, just close your eyes and relax. I'll be here, I'll always be here."

"Diana..I ..." I held her hand tightly and closed my eyes as I was overcome with emotion.

Just then a Nurse rushed into the room. "The monitor sounded an alarm in our station. Your vitals are spiking! You have to relax! Mrs. Palazzo, you're going to have to leave the room for a while!"

As she spoke, I passed out again. I don't know when I left my body, but I did and I was in another place, standing at the base of a huge waterfall.

"Come with me; it's time to go," the voice said.

"Please, I beg of you, just one more chance? I have to talk to her."

I awoke to an empty room. I looked around at all the medical equipment and realized I was indeed lucky. The stress of my life had caught up with me and seeing Diana filled my glass. I laid there and pondered my fate. The following days passed slowly and I was eventually taken out of ICU and placed in a private room. While I sat there for days I had plenty of time to think about my fate, Diana's fate, and our future. Although Diana was visiting me daily, I had to wait until I was stronger to talk to her. It wouldn't be easy but it had to be done.

After a month in the hospital I had to say goodbye to Diana for a while. I was sent home to Porter Ranch, Ca. via an ambulance. Phyllis still lived in our house as the divorce wasn't final yet. She took care of me on a daily basis and our relationship began to grow again, albeit slowly. In the process we discovered a newfound respect for each other. I still chatted to Diana on a daily basis and life became stressful again as I was torn between two women, one I had a life with, and one I fantasized about having a life with.

I also spent a lot of time with my children and my six grandchildren, knowing my days may be numbered, knowing I wasn't promised tomorrow. I visited them at their homes, both out of state and in state. It was with lunch with my middle daughter one day that I reached a realization. While she ate, I sadly looked across the table, studying her, and wondered if she'll be okay when I'm gone, whether her health would hold up. She was the one who developed epilepsy at birth and had been catered to all her life. That's when I realized my soul was dying.

I realized I lived a full life and my spark was gone, along with the no fear attitude I carried for years. I was feeling fear for the first time and just felt I wouldn't be around much longer. Never knowing fear, this grabbed me.

When I got home I sat down and wrote a letter, as Diana was on my mind again.

"Diana,

I liken our time on this planet to a train ride, a long train ride through many peak's and valley's, through sunny days and grey days. We are born on that train at the beginning of our journey. This is when we first meet our parents. As we grow, others step on the train and influence us in one way or another, that be it teachers, clergy, friends, family, etc. As the train makes it's journey through life, some people get on and some get off, sometimes joining us and sometimes leaving us on the train alone. Some are very influential, while others are barely noticeable. Regardless, they are there and influence us along the way whether you realize it or not. The train makes many stops, some through periods of joy, sadness, hellos and goodbyes. Nevertheless it continues and we hopefully learn about life along the way.

The big mystery is this Diana; We don't know when we will step off that train. It is this reason alone we must live in the best way possible and love every minute. Our seat on the train of life will be vacated someday so we must leave behind beautiful memories for the next traveller. We mustn't hurt anyone along the way or we will pay for it later. So Diana, although you think I stepped off your train a long time ago, my spirit has never left you. I am sorry we missed so much of the ride together, but I am here now, maybe not completely, but I'm here when you close your eyes. Nobody knows what lies in store for the rest of our journey or whether I'll be there with you. But right now I have to stay with Phyllis and you have to stay with Pete. Through all of this I discovered I needed Phyllis and you know Pete needs you. We are too old to play with Karma. If this was meant to be it'll happen eventually, so let's put it in God's hands. I want you to know I love you and I always loved you.

You know how we were raised my steel town girl; you knew my family and I knew yours. The iron ore, coal dust and soot from that steel mill town we came from runs through our veins like steel coils in a spring. It gave us a grit that's indescribable. We were hometown kids and walked the same streets and went to the same schools. We walked the hills of that valley when the newly fallen snow was dirty from soot, and listened to the screeching trains that kept us awake at night. When the roar from the blast furnace lit up the night sky it lit up our senses too. You were my sun in the morning and my moon at night. The dream we had of being together forever never materialized, but I'm telling you the dream was real and was needed at the time. It wasn't a fantasy because it played out in my mind everyday when I was imprisoned and it still does. To me if it wasn't real I wouldn't be here today. Though we are separated by thousands of miles, I wouldn't be lying if I told you you are always on my mind.

And remember this Diana; A loss of a Love just doesn't go away; you never forget it. It eats on you every day. It's a loss as big as death, only worse. There is no closure, it stays with you.

And because of this, part of me will always be with you.

Addio All'amore Diana,

Pasquale"

After writing her, the phone rang; it was Diana. I was surprised because she had never called me before.

"Pasquale, how are you?"
"I'm fine Diana, what a surprise! Are you okay? You never call."

"Pasquale, there's been something I've wanted to tell you, but it seems I never had the chance. it's killing me! Our time in Tahoe went by too quickly and then you had to go. I have to be sure you're okay before I talk to you."

"Okay, I'm fine. What is it? What's so important? Are you okay?"

"Damn it Pasquale, I'm fine. Listen to me! You have a son! There's no other way to tell you! You have a son! Vincenzo was born nine months after we saw each other at Niagara Falls. I tried to tell you in Tahoe a few times, but never really got the opportunity. We were so rapt up with each other, then you got sick and I couldn't. I was afraid the news would have been hard on your heart. As I look back on it, I'm sorry I didn't tell you."

I sat there stunned. Vincenzo? So many questions went through my mind. Where do I start?

"Diana, I'm shocked! After all these years! Oh my God, what does that make him, 49 years old? Oh my God!"

"Yes Pasquale, and he looks and acts so much like you."

"Does he know about me? Does he know anything about me?"

"Yes Pasquale, he knows all about you. He knows everything about you. He lives in San Francisco and he wants to meet you as soon as you feel better. When I told him of our meeting, we both cried on the phone. He really wants to see you."

"Wow, I'm shocked! Why didn't you tell me?"

"Pasquale, our reunion went by so quickly and we were bombarded with feelings. I wanted to tell you, but because of your condition I couldn't. I thought it was safe to do it now."

"Diana, let me digest this, okay? I am so happy, yet I am so sad. He grew up without me, and I him. Let me get back to you soon, okay?"

"Okay Pasquale, I want you to know I love you; we both love you."

"I love you too Diana......and please say hello to him for me. Please tell him I'm happy and doing fine."

I hung up, closed my eyes and smiled. I tried to relax but Diana and Vincenzo filled my mind; that and the fact I have to tell Phyllis somehow.

Chapter Eleven

Phyllis's only knowledge of Diana was what I told her years ago, when we first met. She knew I was looking for her and that I found her in Lake Tahoe, the home of our Time-share. She didn't know the thought of her consumed my mind for years. Yes, we were getting a divorce, but thinking she would understand that I looked for Diana and found her after all these years might topple the glass, making it impossible to repair. And Vincenzo! How will she accept that? God, the thought of this was suffocating.

Although we were consciously making an effort at reconciliation, there was an undercurrent that ripped through my soul. So many questions! Did she want to get back together because she felt sorry for me after my heart attack? Was I growing attached to her because she was caring for me? Did we truly love each other or was being together a habit based on convenience? Am I "settling" because of my age? Is she "settling" for security? Will she be alright if I leave, knowing we're up in age now? Damn, I care about her but the passion is gone; I feel more like a roommate. These and many other feelings filled my mind.

I was still confined to a chair all day with a minimum amount of exercise. I watched Phyllis care for my needs and go about her daily chores in the house, all the time waiting for an opportunity to talk to her. She was as wrapped up in her daily life as I was wrapped up in Diana. We occupied the same space but communication was rare.

As I sat there in my chair I perused the room, a room full of my past. Photos of our wedding day were on one wall. On another were photos of our kids and grandkids. Then there was another wall, a tribute to my years in the service.

The photo of my enlistment in Air Force blues from the waist up; no one knowing we were in our underwear from the waist down and being herded through the photography area like cattle. A proud photo of me at Flight School Graduation, a photo of me in flight gear standing next to my F-4 Phantom, and then my Service Medal's reminding me of more somber times. All of this consumed me as I pondered the thought of leaving this life behind. After all, this house was where we raised our kids; what would they think? Would they judge me?

Would they think I'm abandoning their mother? Would they accept Diana? What would our grandkids grow up believing?

The start of a new life at my age is daunting and perhaps foolish. It is literally quite scary. You weigh your options, you try to balance the scale with good points and bad points. You weigh everything, knowing at my age there might not be a tomorrow. Realizing this, you proceed cautiously. Should I stay in my comfort zone with sex once in a while, but without love, or do I gamble on a new life with a fantasy that has consumed me for years. Gambling stirs the senses and brings new excitement and perhaps new love, but it also brings new baggage. Will she accept mine, and will I accept hers? Will she be what I want and need and vice versa. I've spent all my life trying to be happy; being a visual man and not deep enough is a problem I've tried to overcome. I realized I truly am broken.

Vincenzo! Now that's another story all together. Wow, a son that grew up without me! I closed my eyes and pondered that for a long time. I sense and know that he was raised properly, but without a father how proper can it get? Sure, he had a step-father who filled in for me, and knowing Diana I'm quite sure he treated

Vincenzo well. But I wasn't there and I felt guilty about that. He's almost 50 now, a grown man with perhaps grandchildren of his own. Wow, that put me back in the moment. It's too late to feel sorry and it's too late to try to change things. I must accept him for the man he grew to be and hopefully he will accept me. It gave me comfort to know that he knows I didn't abandon him, that I was taken out of his life by extraordinary circumstances. For that reason alone I feel he will accept me.

And then there's Phyllis and Pete. I've known the woman I'm with for 40 years, while I've had feelings for Diana since we were kids . I've fantasized for years to finally be with her, but here we are, me married for 40 years and her married for 44 years. True love has no limits to what it will do or wait for, but it seems life has been cruel. Phyllis and I started divorce proceedings and though they're in limbo, they could be reinitiated at any time. Pete is gravely ill with who knows how much time he has to live. What to do?

Chapter Twelve

Days went by with my mind muddled. Being Italian though, I always wore my emotions on my sleeve. Phyllis knew that and confronted me one afternoon after I got off the phone. I guess I let my guard down, or perhaps I didn't care.

"Can you tell me who calls you every day? You seemed so engrossed, and your mood changes drastically after each phone call. You're grouchy one minute and then you're happy. What's going on? Who calls you?"

"Phyllis, I don't know how to tell you, but I'm going to make it straight, I owe you that."

I was tense as Phyllis sat on the couch across the room and stared at me. I didn't know where to start, so I figured I better start at the beginning.

"Phyllis, I've been a lonely man for a long time. Oh, don't get me wrong, it's not you, it's me. I'm broken inside. When the kids left home and started out on their own is when it all began. But maybe it started long ago, long before you met me. It started in that hell hole in

Vietnam when I was in solitary confinement for six years. I learned there how to compartmentalize things to keep me sane. One of the things that kept me sane back then was my love for Diana. When they used to beat me and torture me I would close my eyes and she'd be there. She kept me alive. I know I told you about her years ago, but I only glossed over the surface. I loved her immensely. When I was released I used to park outside her house and relive our memories. I tried in vain to find her but I couldn't.

After a futile few months I moved to California. When I met you I felt alive again, but I never forgot her. There was no closure. I always wondered what happened to her, if she was okay, etc.

After the kids left home and you were engrossed in your life is when I felt alone again. It's probably not your fault. I shouldn't rely on you for my happiness, it has to come from within, but it never did. That's when we agreed to a divorce. After the divorce proceedings started I searched a couple of dating sites looking for God knows what. I foolishly thought I would find happiness that way, but like I said, you can't make someone else make you happy. Then one day at work, todays date popped up on my computer and I realized it was Diana's birthday. That's when I got obsessed again with finding her. I felt that since we were getting divorced it was okay to do so. I felt like I wasn't cheating on you. After striking out many times, with the help of the computer, I found her in Lake Tahoe, Incline Village to be exact.

Phyllis began to squirm in her chair. She looked at me in disbelief and crossed her arms on her chest.

"Incline Village," she yelled! How long have you been communicating with her? Is she the reason you filed for divorce? "

"I just recently found her, after we filed for divorce... and NO, she's not the reason. Her memory popped up one day at work after we filed."

"How long was she living there? Do you mean we went there for years and she was in the same town? That town isn't that big, you probably knew she lived there when you purchased the Condo, didn't you? I don't believe a word you're saying. I don't believe in coincidences."

Her demeanor changed from curious to angry, as I interrupted her.

"No, I swear! This was a complete coincidence. Maybe, just maybe, we somehow were drawn to the same place? I was shocked too she was living there. But there's more..."

Then she interrupted me again.

"So, this is why you were in Incline Village when you had your heart attack? You son of a bitch! What were you doing? Screwing her?"

"You're disgusting," she said, as she got up and left the room.

I sat there staring at the door she exited, suffocated by the sudden silence and the thoughts going through my mind. I knew she wouldn't take this easily, but I've always been honest, brutally honest at times, it was my nature. Then she came storming back into the room.

"Pasquale, you're not going to hurt me anymore. I put up with your PTSD for years and the hollow look in your eyes; the kids did too. I tried for years to make you happy but you're scarred too deeply. You really hurt me now. I mistakenly thought we could make it this time, but I was wrong. You betrayed me! You snuck behind my back and I'm done, I'm totally done."

There weren't any tears, just a matter of factness that represented her feelings. I guess too much water had passed under our bridge for her to cry. I felt terrible inside. I had feelings too and part of me still loved her. You don't close a book on a 40 year relationship easily.

"I'm sorry Phyllis, I really am. I just can't explain my feelings."

Phyllis wasn't done yet. She pointed her finger at me....

"If you think you can leave here and explore your fantasy and I'll be waiting for you after reality smacks you in the face you're wrong. You go do what you got to do. But I'm telling you I'm gone too. We're finished. I can't believe you had the nerve to tell me you've been thinking of her for forty years, the forty years we were married. I'll never forget that. You betrayed me Pasquale, you betrayed me."

Then the tears fell. She put her hands to her face and sobbed uncontrollably. I looked at her and couldn't speak; I felt helpless. I just watched her, almost void of feelings. The clock had struck midnight for us and our "perfect" marriage had collapsed. The cat was out of the bag. I felt it was all my doing, but I also felt I was a victim here too, as I wasn't in control of my feelings. Then she looked at me again.

"You're a fool, that's what you are. Your mind thinks she's still seventeen, but wait, you'll see.

The petals have fallen off the rose and with it comes brand new baggage."

"Phyllis, I've been trying to tell you I have a son, a son! She had him nine months after our last meeting, before I went to Vietnam. This plays on my mind terribly, knowing he was raised without me. I don't even know him!"

"What!!!! When did you find this out? In Lake Tahoe? What else don't I know about?"

"She is married, but her husband is on life support. She lives alone and waits for the phone to ring, a phone call notifying her of his death. And you're right, you're right about everything. I'm not twenty-one and she isn't seventeen. There is baggage. I have a son I never knew, a son I never saw. Isn't there any compassion in you at all? Can't you see the dilemma I'm in?"

"How do you know the son is yours and not just a ploy to win you back? Have you thought about that?"

"I know he is! I believe her! It was the way she told me. She didn't tell me until after I got home from the hospital. She didn't want to excite me further."

"Well, it looks like you dug yourself a hole this time Casanova. It looks like we're done here. If you want to pursue her, go ahead."

"You don't get it. She's married and I would never do that to a man on life support. I just want to see my son."

"Oh Pasquale, do you think I'm stupid? You were pursuing her before you knew you had a son. She was always on your mind. This is only icing on the cake for you now. You do what you got to do.....I'm done, the glass is full. My wall is built. You're not going to hurt me anymore."

Phyllis left the room, grabbed her keys and drove off in haste. I stood up and watched her drive away into the rain. I was overrun with guilt. To alleviate my stress I poured myself two fingers of Scotch and sat at my desk and wrote a letter to Diana, perhaps to communicate, or perhaps to ease my mind. After all, it always worked before!

"Dear Diana,

The clock has struck twelve here. My coach has turned into a pumpkin. Phyllis confronted me, forcing me to tell her about you. She wanted to know who calls me daily and why my mood changes after the call. I was never good at lying, so I told her everything. I spilled the beans regarding my feelings for you and how long I've had them. It was a mea culpa. I'm sad

now and yet I'm glad. A myriad of motions are going through me as I think of you and her. We were separated by hands of fate and Phyllis provided the love I needed for years. I am torn between the two of you. Why? Oh why does life have to be so tough, so complicated? I pray nightly, hoping God will help me through this. Whatever happens, I believe God will help me. I left it in his hands as it is too much for me to carry.....although today's events might have been the deciding factor. The ball may be going too fast to slow down now. The complicated situation may be out of my hands. Todays events might be the coup de grace'.
Pasquale"

Chapter Thirteen

So here I am, 72 years old, divorcing a woman I was married to for 40 years and having to try to start a new life. It was 2 months short of our 41 year wedding anniversary and I felt like a heel. We were parents to five beautiful children and six grandchildren. They would be in shock if they found out. We had kept it from them purposely.

I had been in contact with Diana since I left Lake Tahoe and she was aware of my situation. She was awesome for moral support and helped me through my periods of loneliness. But I couldn't contact her now. This was something I'll have to face myself. Damn, life is cruel I thought.

I spent the rest of the day and evening watching TV and medicating myself with Scotch on the rocks. I was getting ready for bed when the doorbell rang. It was ten o'clock and highly unusual. I put my robe on, turned on the lights and stumbled down the stairs to the door. I opened it to surprisingly find a Deputy Sheriff Standing there in the rain.

"Mr. Cipriano?"

"Yes. Is there something wrong?"

"Mr. Cipriano, your wife has been involved in a serious car accident."

I stood there dumbfounded. My mind was racing.

"What happened? Is she okay?"

"She was T-boned at a traffic light in Simi Valley and thrown from her vehicle. She is at Memorial Hospital on Sycamore in Simi Valley. I can't tell you anything further."

"Oh my God! Is she alive? When did this happen?"

Mr. Cipriano, it happened about an hour ago. I suggest you go there as soon as possible. She was in serious condition. That's all I know."

"I appreciate you coming here. Thank you. I'm on my way."

I ran upstairs and threw some clothes on. I got in my car and raced to the hospital. It was still raining and the roads were slick. My mind was racing, my heart was pounding. The hospital was twenty minutes from my house but it seemed like an eternity. I had been drinking and hoped I didn't get stopped. I didn't realize how much I loved her until now. Our forty years of marriage ran through my mind, every good moment it seemed. I was overcome with guilt from our last conversation, thinking perhaps this was why she got hurt, that perhaps if she wasn't mad she might have seen the oncoming car.

I parked at the emergency room and ran in. I explained who I was and what happened. Then the wait began. I couldn't see her, she was in the Operating Room. I couldn't sit so I paced the floor. I called my kids and told them what happened. My oldest daughter took it the hardest, but no one lived close by. I had no one to lean on.

Time went by and I rehashed everything again. It seemed like hours before a Doctor and Nurse came out to talk to me. They looked glum. I looked up at the fluorescent lights on the ceiling and cried "No God, no!"

"Mr. Cipriano?"

"Yes, how is she? Is she okay?"

"Please, come with me. Let's go to my office to talk."

I stared at him, then at the nurse.

"Why can't you tell me here? What's going on? How is she?"

I was panicking and I knew it. My chest began to hurt, so I reached in my pocket for my

Nitro and put one under my tongue. A rush went through my head and the pain subsided. The Doctor grabbed my shoulders and looked me in the eyes.

"Are you alright Mr. Cipriano?"

"I don't know, I just had a quadruple bypass a little over two months ago and I get weak. I have to sit down. This is all too sudden."

After I sat down, he called for a gurney and I was whisked into the Emergency Room for tests. The Doctor patted me on my shoulder and told me to relax, told me that she was still alive. This relieved me momentarily. I closed my eyes and said a prayer. I didn't know if I was dying; I didn't know if Phyllis was dying.

As I lay there they did many tests, an EKG which was normal and blood tests which proved normal. They gave me a sedative and I then awoke in a hospital room all by myself. I pushed the Nurse's button because I needed information, both about me and Phyllis. I felt like my world was tumbling down and I had no control. I was on a roller coaster of emotional bedlam. Yes, I was sedated but my mind was still working.

A few minutes later a Nurse came into the room. I was comforted to find out my heart was fine and I just experienced a panic attack. I was on a low grade tranquilizer and would receive another in a few hours.

"Can you tell me anything about my wife? She was involved in a terrible traffic accident. She's in this hospital."

"Yes, we know Mr. Cipriano. However we can't disclose any information. That would have to come from her Doctor. He has been notified. Are you okay? Can I get you anything?"

"I want to know how my wife is! Can't you tell me anything, anything at all?"

"I'm sorry Mr. Cipriano, we really don't know anything either....patient confidentiality you know! I wish I could help. Would you like some juice or something?"

"No, please get the Doctor up here, okay?"

The Nurse left the room. I looked at the clock on the wall and it was four in the morning. I must have slept after the tranquilizer. My mind was rushing again. At five thirty the Doctor came into the room.

"Mr. Cipriano, my name is Dr. Sall. I'm the Neurosurgeon that operated on your wife."

I lay there and let him speak.

"Your wife suffered a broken hip, shoulder and a traumatic brain injury. She is in ICU as we speak. Mr. Cipriano, her condition is grave. She had a fractured skull which produced subdural hematomas and intracerebral hemorrhages. These produced intracranial pressure which required surgery. When brain swelling is particularly severe, elevated pressure can only be relieved temporarily by surgically removing a portion of the skull. This we had to do. This allowed swollen tissues to bulge out reducing the risk for pressure-induced damage. To manage this condition, we inserted a device called an ICP monitor through the skull to provide us with a constant pressure reading. If the ICP rises too high, we'll have to administer medications to draw fluid out of the brain and into blood vessels, decreasing the brain's metabolic requirements, and increasing blood flow to the injured tissues. She is also placed on a ventilator to ensure an adequate supply of oxygen (hyperventilation), which is necessary to promote healing. A buildup of fluid inside the brain is also a concern in acute treatment for TBI. If the fluid-containing spaces in the brain (ventricles) experience blockage, I'll have to insert a tube called a shunt to drain the fluid buildup (hydrocephalus). This will allow the ventricles to shrink and restore normal function to brain cells. Elevated ICP due to swelling, hydrocephalus, or blood clots significantly impacts recovery from TBI. We also had to put her in a self induced coma. All these steps are being taken. Her prognosis at the time is poor. I'm sorry, but we're doing everything we can."

"Can I see her Doc?"

"We can let you see her from the doorway, but a bacterial infection to the brain is a real fear at the moment. Like I said, her condition is grave. Most edema subsides within a few days or weeks, but a few minutes or hours of excessive ICP can cause permanent damage."

He helped me out of bed and called an Orderly and a wheelchair to walk me down the hall to the elevators. I was glum and could't speak. My future and past played out in my mind. We got off at Level 5 and was let into the ICU Ward. When we reached the room she was in I could see her through the glass from the hallway. She was unrecognizable. All bandaged up in a body cast, IV tubes going to her arms and her head was bandaged to prevent infection. Knowing part of her skull was removed and her brain was exposed made my stomach queasy. I stared at her, looked up to the ceiling and said a prayer. Then I recalled the discussion we had before she left the house in anger and felt responsible again. A tear rolled down my cheek as I reflected on the good times we shared.

"Doc, what is her prognosis? Will she ever be okay?"

"If she does make it there is a chance her motor capabilities will be impaired. She might never be the same. The next 24 hours is key. We are doing everything we can."

I asked them to wheel me back to my room. I needed some time by myself. I was overwhelmed with emotion. The kids! I have to contact the kids. I knew they'd want to know. Everyone was somber when they heard the news and they wanted to come to the hospital. I knew they all lived a good distance away, but who was I to tell them no. We have always been a family and their response was expected. They were on the way.

We all have our favorites. We shouldn't, but human nature as it is always seems to dictate our terms. Phyllis was always closest to her youngest daughter Dina, a practical realist if you ever saw one, although she had moments of passion when inspired. Tammy lived about three hours away at the beach in southern California with her husband and beautiful son Robby, while the rest were two to three hours away too.....except for Michael, who live in Texas. Nevertheless, they were coming home to see their mom.

Chapter Fourteen

Meanwhile, it was Spring in the mountains and a seasonal storm was pounding the Sierra's. Diana stood at her picture window with a cup of coffee in her hand and stared at the majestic and serene winter wonderland before her eyes. She wanted to go to the local Casino but the snow storm changed that idea. She had heard from Pasquale a couple of hours ago and was told about the conversation he had with Phyllis. She didn't know the complete conversation but somehow felt responsible for their breakup. Her birthday was approaching and wished Pasquale was there to share it with her.

   Life hasn't been easy for her. She believed she lost her first lover years ago during the war. Then she marries a man who becomes a CIA Operative and lived in anxiety the next forty years, never knowing if and when he'd be killed. The phone call in the middle of the night from the Director telling her about his being wounded in Afghanistan and his condition was like a nail in the coffin. Then her staying in

Washington to be there for him was traumatic too; she had watched a proud man reduced to a vegetable. When hope was lost, she reluctantly went home to Tahoe and waited. For what? Another phone call? It seems she's waited for bad phone calls all her life.

She held the warm cup in her hand and stared at the creamy liquid and went to another place, far away, to another time when life was peaceful. Oh Tahoe, what a beautiful place it has been, a retreat from anxiety and the real world. An escape from reality at times is what it is. The crystal clear cobalt water surrounded by the snowy, majestic Sierra's is truly captivating. She remembered when she hiked a different location every week, when she learned how to ski at Heavenly Valley and Rose Mountain, when she kayaked the lake in the summer, and where her and Pete dined at the various Italian restaurants in the Reno Tahoe area. Life seemed simple then. She was in love again.

It was also Tahoe that helped her forget about Pasquale and the good times they had growing up. Campbell, Ohio, was a distant place now. She went back a couple of times for High School reunions and it wasn't the same. The town was ravaged with famine after the mills closed, even her grade school and high school were razed. She reflected driving through the cemetery and noticing all the ethnic names on the tombstones, names of families she knew but are gone, ethnic names you don't see in California or Nevada. It seems everything is gone now. Thinking of that only depressed her further. Thank God for the friends she still embrace, friends she's known for over 50 years.

As she went to the kitchen to refresh her coffee cup, the phone rang. She stared at it annoyingly, the noise blaring in the quiet house. She always hated when the phone rang.

"Hello."

"Diana, it's me. Can we talk or are you busy?"

"I'm not busy Pasquale, I was just thinking of you. You don't sound good, are you alright?"

"Diana, I really need to talk to you now. Phyllis and I had an argument after we last talked and she left in a huff. Two hours later a cop comes to the door and tells me she'd been in a traffic accident and is hospitalized. It doesn't look good."

"My God, what happened? What do you mean it doesn't look good?"

"Diana, she has massive head trauma and multiple injuries. They had to open her skull because of pressure caused by edema. She's in a self induced coma at the moment."

"What can I do Pasquale? Do you want me to come there for you?"

"That is a nice thought, but it wouldn't be wise at the moment. All the kids are on their way here to see her. I told them it was serious. Just be there for me, okay? I really need you now."

"Whether you know it or not Pasquale, I've always been here for you. Call me anytime you want, okay? I'm here for you. Call me any time."

They said their goodbyes and Diana walked back to the window and stared at the snow. It wasn't beautiful anymore. It was a cold, white canvas covered with both gloom and optimism. Her mind was in fourth gear and accelerating rapidly. She wondered if Phyllis would make it and whether her accident would make them closer again. She wondered how she was going to tell Pasquale about her business. Then she spun a one-eighty and imagined her and Pasquale together one day, with Phyllis and Pete both gone and without the guilt of a break-up. She walked into the bedroom and brushed her hair, put some makeup on and grabbed her coat and keys. Bad weather or not, she was going to the Hyatt Casino down the road. She had to get out of this lonely house. She needed a drink.

She also didn't feel like being alone; the hum of the Casino always made her forget reality.

Chapter Fifteen

Pasquale sat in his hospital bed and watched the eleven o'clock news. His mind was racing, even though he was sedated. The kids wouldn't be here until morning; he had to put up a strong front. Out of habit, he asked for a pen and paper. He had to write Diana; it always comforted him.

"Dear Diana,

Life is a blur to me right now. As you love Pete, I love Phyllis. Previously, she became someone I convinced myself I no longer knew or got along with because I never gave her the time and affection and attention she craved. I thought I gave it to her, but when I really thought about it I never really did. I never really gave her a chance. Mentally, I had ended my marriage years before with the simple and cold decision that she was no longer who or what I wanted. But so much has transpired in the last few months since we found each other. I was ready to leave her, to start anew, but tonight's accident has my head spinning and reminiscing. Before tonight, we slowly got to know each other again, the new people we became over time. But I changed all that tonight and I feel guilty about what happened. I wish you were here to comfort me.

Pasquale"

I placed the letter on my nightstand and summoned the nurse so I could take the sleeping pill prescribed. I needed it and I was out in no time at all. With the hospital being what it is, I was awoken twice for my vitals to be taken and once for a blood thinner, each time leaving me grumbling.

I awoke to the sun shining brightly on my pillow. I adjusted the bed to a sitting position and stared out the window. "What a beautiful day," I thought! Just as my breakfast was delivered the phone rang; it was Pasquale. Everyone was downstairs except for Michael, who was enroute from the airport. They asked if it was okay to come up. Their mom was in ICU and because of her condition couldn't have visitors. Our reunion was bittersweet. I'm in a hospital bed and their mom is in ICU; their visit had to be painful. I tried to keep the conversation light, trying to alleviate their apprehension.

After a couple days, the Doctor discharged me to my kids. We spent quality time together, as time seemed valuable now and for some reason I felt I was staring mortality in the face. I told them about my conversation with Phyllis before her accident and how it adversely affected me, of how I realized how much I loved her. They all took it well except for Dina, her favorite. I could tell she was bitter about my newfound relationship.

We spent our days together talking, reminiscing and visiting the hospital to peer through the glass at their mom in ICU. Before they left we ate out often and spent time cooking together at dinner. Then one day the phone rang. Phyllis expired.

I put the phone down and sat down in shock. I'm not stupid. I was aware of her condition and thought I was mentally prepared for the news, but I soon found out that thinking about it and living through it are two different things. The old adage about the Bullfighter went through my mind....."everyone goes to the Bullfight and screams suggestions on how to kill the Bull.....but only one man fights the Bull," and today it was me.

I sat there and reached for my bottle of nitro in my pocket. I felt a loss that was incomprehensible. I stared at the TV in front of me, even though it was off at the moment. The screen revealed our 40 yrs together, the good and the bad. I stared, and with tears in my eyes, I relived it all. I must have sat in that chair for an hour before I picked up the phone and acted strong in front of my kids. One by one, they accepted the news, some with shock, some with a pragmatism instilled from within. I asked Pasquale to handle the Funeral arrangements, as I knew I couldn't think straight.

Her Funeral was attended by many. Days went by and then weeks and months. Diana had called me many times but our conversation was always short. I was in a funk, a tunnel that kept winding, but then one day the sun appeared. It came in a letter from Diana.

"Pasquale,

I know the loss of your wife has affected you badly and I'm sorry. But I have to tell you Pete passed away two weeks ago and I feel your pain. What comforts me is knowing he isn't in pain anymore. Although you and Phyllis were closer than Pete and I, the loss is still the same. It leaves a void in your heart that may never be filled again. I don't know where we stand

116

anymore, but I still feel a connection with you, a connection I'd like to pursue. Please get in touch with me. I've been very busy the last two weeks. I've tried to call you, but couldn't reach you.

Here Always,
Diana"

I called her immediately and gave my condolences, knowing firsthand the pain she suffered. I was better at comforting others than comforting myself. We became Facebook friends and e-mailed each other regularly. We sent messages to each other all day and night. Although our love was growing, I wanted to stay in California until the time was right. But it seemed Diana was my future; Diana was who I should have been with all along. It was a cruel hand of fate that separated us and it was a cruel hand of fate that brought us back together.

May came along and her birthday was approaching. She called me and thought we should celebrate it since it's been years since we had. I again realized that I missed the woman I first fell in love with. I also realized that if I'd treated Phyllis the way I'd treated Diana, and used the hours I spent with her on my mind, we'd have made it and she may not have been killed. It was a cruel paradox.

Chapter Sixteen

Tahoe was an eight hour drive from Simi
Valley. I decided to take the scenic route up Rt
395 past Bishop and Mammoth, absorbing the
geological features. Aside from being pretty and
longer to travel, the drive had far less traffic than
US-99 or I-5. I enjoyed the view and the
meditation it offered. There was so much to
think about. Phyllis had been dead for a year
and Pete just died. The snow capped Sierra's in
the distance reminded me of our first meeting in
Tahoe. We have been apart our whole life and
have developed traits and quirks that may be
offensive to each other. We are different people
now; will we get along? This is definitely going
to be an experience in acceptance.

Diana had a multi million dollar home on the
lake and I arrived there around five in the
evening. As I traveled down her long driveway
I was surprised there were two Mercedes'
parked out front. Diana met me at the door with
a kiss and introduced me to two beautiful
women in their late twenties or early thirties.

They were dressed very fashionably with sweaters, tight pants and heels, designer clothes and purses all. Diana introduced us and poured me a drink while she answered her phone and walked out of the room to talk. While she was on the phone we made small talk. After a few minutes they stood up and said they had to leave. They said it'll be getting dark soon and they had to go to Reno over Mount Rose. I watched Diana walk them to their cars and hand then an envelope and some business cards while they talked outside.

When she came in I asked her who they were, as they were very young, attractive and driving Benz convertibles. She looked at me like she expected a question and laughed it off, saying they belong to the Bridge Club downtown.

"I was giving them the schedule for our next few months."

"I just wondered; I didn't know you played Bridge!"

"Pasquale, there's a lot you don't know about me!"

"Okay, I could buy that, and vice versa I guess."

She looked at me like she wanted to say something, but quickly turned away.

"Well, tomorrow is your birthday, how would you like to spend it," I asked?

"There's a cute little Piano Bar down in Sparks at The Nugget. It has a peaceful and romantic setting. I thought we could have dinner there, reminisce and share old times, you know, get to know each other better. We have so much to share."

It was evening in the mountains and getting cool when the sun went down. We went down the road to the Hyatt for dinner and played some video poker at the bar we first met at, almost a year and a half ago. When we got home I got some firewood and started a fire. We both stood there in front of the fireplace and hugged while the fire got warm.

That's not all that got warm. The fire, our closeness, the ambience took over. As she kissed me she put her hand in my trousers and pulled me and my penis over to the couch. She pushed me down on the couch and started to undress in front of me. Ever so slowly she took off her clothes, her red sweater first, then her tight black slacks, leaving her heels on. She took off her black laced bra and faced me, exposing beautifully sculptured breasts, a plastic surgeon's creation. Then she turned around and took off her black laced thong, bending over exposing a well rounded tight ass. As she undressed I unbuttoned my shirt and my belt as she got down on her knees in front of me. She grabbed me by my the back of my neck and pulled me to her, kissing me, my tongue being sucked ever so softly. Her perfume was mesmerizing, making my head spin with excitement. Then she kissed my neck, my nipples and slid her tongue down my body until she enveloped me in her warm mouth, her tongue dancing in circles. As I sat there and watched this beautiful woman, I couldn't help but think of the years we missed together.

"Come here baby," I said, "That's enough. I don't want to explode without pleasing you too."

While on her knees, I pulled her up to me with my hands cupped around her tight ass and kissed her wet mouth. Then I stood up while she enveloped me in her again, her warm mouth so warm, so inviting. I grabbed her head in my hands and pulled her up to me, with both of us standing. Then I lifted her leg and brought it home ever so slowly, teasing her while she put her arms around my neck and kissed me passionately. With one hand holding her back and the other cupped around her ass, I thrust it into her deeply while she let out a passionate moan, sucking my tongue, breathing hard and deep. Being consumed by the moment, i lifted her up off the ground with her legs wrapped around me. As I held her she grinded on me and sucked my tongue hard, letting out a moan that made me thrust deeper.

"My God, I could feel you in my stomach," she murmured. Pasquale, take me, take me! You feel so fucking good."

As she slowly ground on me, her soft, yet firm hips swaying in a poetic motion, I walked over to the Bear rug near the fireplace and bent down to my knees and laid her down ever so gently. She kissed me in a way I never thought possible while I entertained her beautiful breasts, rubbing her nipples with my thumb until they became erect.

"I don't want us ever to forget this moment," I said.

She answered me by pulling my head to her and sucked my tongue again, her wet mouth quivering with her body in unison. We both exploded in wonderful pain. I screamed aloud when I came, while she moaned incoherently. It was wonderful. Although it only lasted a few minutes, It was the best sex I ever had.

We lay there for awhile, both hugging and enjoying the heat from the fire. We talked for awhile and then she slid her hand down and grabbed my balls and started to caress them.

"I don't think so hon, I'm not that young anymore," I said.

"Trust me, you have one more left."

Then she stood up between me and the fireplace, her well sculpted body outlined beautifully in her black nylons and heels she still wore.

"You stay right there, I'll be right back," she said as she gracefully stepped over me. She went to the kitchen and came back smiling.

"Now where were we," she said, as she stood between me and the glowing fire. "Oh yeah, I remember."

Then she kneeled between my legs and got on her elbows with her cute ass up in the air, her shape being defined by the warm yellow fire glowing behind her. I looked down at her pretty face while she enveloped me in her mouth again. But then a strange sensation came over me....she had ice in her mouth and her tongue was swirling it around my head ...cold than warm, cold then warm. Then she started licking and sucking my balls while she caressed my ass with her long fingernails and stroked me with her other hand. I couldn't believe what was happening..."Damn, this girl is good," I thought!

When she started sucking on me again I exploded. She swallowed and devilishly smiled at me...."See, I knew you could!" I pulled her up to me and kissed her again, tasting my warm juice on her lips and feeling closer than ever.

As we hugged I could feel her breast's against me.

"When did you get the breast job? You look awesome!"

"Oh, about ten years ago. I went down to Beverly Hills and had them done there. I just wanted to feel better about myself. I actually had them done twice...a C-cup first then a year later a D-cup. Glad you like them!

"Well, I do; like I said, you look awesome."

After another Martini, we fell asleep on that bear rug, waking up and going to bed when the fire went out.

Chapter Seventeen

"Happy Birthday beautiful!," I said as she opened her eyes and I kissed her gently. "I made you some breakfast; I got an Omelet, toast and coffee here, sit up!"

Pasquale, what a surprise! You are such a dear," she said as she stretched, letting her sheet drop below her breasts.

"Well good morning to you too," as I bent over to kiss her nipples.

She sat up in bed and sipped on her coffee while smiling at me, knowing her breast's were exposed.

"Oh Pasquale, I'm so happy we found each other."

"Me too baby. You are such a tease! What do you want to do today?"

"I have to go to Reno to meet a couple of friends for lunch; you're free to come along if you want. They're the two girls you met yesterday."

"Okay, what time we leaving? There's a storm coming in this afternoon and Mount Rose will be hazardous tonight."

"Well we could leave at eleven and be there easily at noon, have lunch and return by four. Is that okay? By the way, Vincenzo is arriving tonight for my birthday and to spend the weekend with us."

"Wow, glad to hear. I'll finally meet him. That works for me Dee. Enjoy your breakfast, I'm going to go get gas. "I'll be right back."

The sky was getting cloudy and the wind was blowing in a front; you could feel the moisture in the air. As I made it up to the Chevron station on Village St., I couldn't help but think how lucky I was to have found her. After all these years and the miles we traveled, the train of life brought us back together, albeit in a cruel way; we were still back together.

I filled up my car and drove to her home admiring the mountains and lake in the distance. How turbulent the lake looked when a front comes in. The usually quiet lake had white caps today as the wind increased.

When I got home Diana was in the shower. I gazed lovingly at her through the glass doors while she blew me a kiss. Then I went to the Great Room and stared at the fireplace while she got ready. Yes, the house still had a dominant male's influence, but it was beautiful nonetheless. While sitting there I noticed a journal on the coffee table and curiously opened it. Inside was documentation of business transactions with several different women, which really made me quizzical. When I heard her heels coming down the hallway I closed the book.

"I'm ready Pasquale, are you ready to go," she asked as she noticed me standing near the journal on the table.

"I am, just been waiting for you. My you look pretty...pink is definitely your color."

"Well thank you! Let's go then."

We both were quiet as we gotten the car. I was trying to figure out what I saw in the journal and I could sense she was wondering what I saw.

The driver over Mount Rose is beautiful to say the least. The road to the summit is mostly straight from Incline Village, but once you reach the 10,800' summit the two lane road turns into a multitude of hairpins as it descend into Reno. From the summit you can see Lake Tahoe to the west, Reno to the east and Carson City to the south, a magnificent view of at least 50 miles in each direction. You can tell there was a front coming in as it was cloudy and the wind was blowing hard at the top of the mountain. We made small talk as we passed the Mount Rose Ski Resort and the Highway Departments storage facility for road salt and their snow plows. The facility was at about 6500' and the drivers of the plows would have to climb the mountain to get to their trucks and snow plows. It appeared we were both avoiding what was on our mind.

We passed Reno and headed to the Nugget in Sparks, Nevada, a Casino which was opened years ago and is the main tourist attraction in Sparks since The Mustang Ranch was closed 20 years ago. The house's of ill repute simply moved to the outskirts of Carson City, about 50 miles down the road.

When we arrived her two friends were already there and seated. One a blond and one a brunette, both stylishly dressed, their designer clothes accenting their figures beautifully.

"Good afternoon," I said. It looks like Diana only knows beautiful women. Nice to see you again."

They smiled, said thank you, and looked at Diana and wished her a Happy Birthday.

"Diana you look great, one of them said. We're not going to ask you your age."

"You better not," Diana laughed. "I'm not counting anymore."

"I'm sorry," I said, looking at them; "I forgot your names."

"I'm Mary Lou," said the blond, and the brunette said her name was Denise.

I apologized for forgetting their names and said I had a lot on my mind yesterday. We ordered and ate lunch while overlooking the Casino floor. When we finished Diana stood up and said she was going to the powder room and asked Jerri and Denise if they wanted to join her. They smiled and quietly got up and walked away together. I was admiring all three of them as they walked away and couldn't help but think how good Diana looked for her age.

As I sipped on my Rum Martini, I noticed the three of them come out of the restroom and stop for a minute to talk. When they got to the table we ordered another round and made small talk. They both took an envelope out of their purse and gave it to Diana wishing her a Happy Birthday. Diana put them in her purse without opening them, which I thought was a bit unusual.

I looked at my watch and noticed it was 3:00 already and was raining outside. I said we better go, because if it's raining here it's snowing on the mountain. We all agreed and walked out the door, with Diana excusing herself to walk them to their cars. When she returned I asked her what was that all about.

"What do you mean," she asked?

I didn't say anything, figuring anything I might say would come out wrong; sometimes it's better to bite the bullet than light a fire. Besides it looked like she didn't want me in her Kool-aid and what I was thinking was probably wrong anyway.

Chapter Eighteen

As we silently drove through Reno and headed through the forest up Mount Rose, Diana turned to look at me.

"Pasquale, there's something I have to tell you. I don't know how, so I'll just start at the beginning. One of the reasons we moved to the Lake Tahoe area was because Pete was a double agent and doing surveillance of Russian spies. Since he was of slavic origin, he picked up their language easily. My last name isn't Palazzo, it's Kovach. It was changed when we moved here, Social Security Cards and all. Two Russian's were living in the Reno area at the time and they used it as a home base for other Russian spies in the country. The Casino's were a perfect place for laundering money and an excuse for flights in and out of the area. In the process Pete first took them to whore houses in the area and realized he could get more out of them by hiring Escorts, where they could spend more time with them. Little by little, as time went by, he had seven girls working for him here and saw the business was very lucrative, especially in a gambling resort. He also had ten girls working for him in Vegas. The rooms the girls would take them to were bugged in advance for surveillance."

I sat there wide-eyed waiting for the punch line and wondering why she was telling me this. Then it hit me!

She looked at me, searching my eyes and then continued.

"When the spies were all rounded up Pete saw the money that could be made in this profession, and since prostitution was legal in Nevada he set up the business in my name, an LTD, keeping his name clean from the government."

"Does Mary Lou and Denise work for you?"

"Yes they do. I know I lied to you, but I had to at the time. I'm sorry. That's why I'm telling you now. The phone calls, the visit to the powder room, the envelopes, it's all business related. So, what do you think of me now," she asked anxiously?

"I suspected something Diana, but had no idea the extent of this," my mind running wild.

We were climbing Mount Rose as we spoke. As it was raining in Reno, it was snowing here and starting to accumulate. The hair pin turns going up the mountain were slippery and getting worse. We passed the storage yard where the snow plows were located and the lights were on inside. The workers were there but haven't driven out yet to clean the road. After having driven this road for years I knew we were in for trouble at the summit without the road being cleaned. If its snowing here, it's blizzard conditions at the top. I tried to focus on the road, but it seemed my whole world was tumbling down. I couldn't turn around if I wanted to, as I could hardly see oncoming traffic and it was a two lane road. I could feel my chest tightening. It seemed to me that I've been outrunning storms my whole life and now I'm encountering two of them, one physical and one mental. My girlfriend is a Madam! What the hell is happening? The more I thought about it, the worse I felt. The girl of my dreams for years, the girl I had on a pedestal, was involved in something so immoral. How do I compartmentalize this, I thought?

"Is that all you have to say Pasquale, she said quizzically? You don't have any questions?"

"What do you want me to say? I'm proud of you? I'm okay with this? I feel like I don't know you anymore! Sometimes it's better to be silent. I may be offensive if I speak now."

She put her hand on my thigh as I clutched my chest. We were nearing white-out conditions, so I reached in my pocket for a Nitro. The surge of the pill went instantly to my brain and the pain in my chest subsided. The snow was brightly illuminated in my headlights, making it almost impossible to see. I had a hunch we'd have trouble coming back and I was right. We left too late. She continued to talk, almost unaware of the road conditions.

"Pasquale, I'm not a whore, I'm a manager of a legal business. I have a Yellow Page Ad and set the prices and make the arrangements, dinner dates, security, etc. Most of our work is referrals; I don't even know the clients. I make over a hundred grand a month. It's just business! You can get used to that, can't you? Pasquale, I could quit right now if you want and we could travel the world!"

I couldn't look at her, the road conditions were so bad. My brain was racing and I could feel my heart pounding. All the letters I wrote, the letters from the heart, seemed to have been written for nothing now. The girl of my dreams, the one I obsessed over, is not who I imagined. I felt like I didn't know her anymore. I was saddened beyond words.

Then I started to recall some of the letters I wrote and realized they were good for me at the time. They actually got me through the hell I endured, and maybe, just maybe, the letters we write are more meaningful to the writer than the addressee. After all, the words do come from the heart.....pacification I called it. It pacified me to express myself.

Just then a car came sliding around the corner at us, upside-down, plowing a wave of snow that covered my windshield and blinded me. It happened so quickly I couldn't react. The lights in front of me exploded and my lights went out. It was instantaneous.

There was total silence. I wasn't in any pain, but seemed to be in a black vacuum..........

"It's time to go," the voice reverberated again in my ears!

I didn't protest this time. The fight in me was gone! I looked down at my lifeless body and saw my car on the side of a snowy mountain. I could see me and Diana lying there in the car with people starting to assemble. It was here I felt an epiphany; the letters from my heart will be no more and they might have been for naught. After about 10-15 minutes emergency personnel arrived and I watched as they pulled us out of the car. Diana was still breathing and they tended to her first, while covering me with a blanket, as they saw I had transpired. I followed Diana to the hospital in Reno and looked over her as they performed emergency surgery. It seemed like forever, but she entered the ICU with a good prognosis........she was going to live!

My funeral was large. I watched my girls weep and my sons remain stoic. So many friends I hadn't seen in years attended. I watched it all. It was as if I never left, as if I was in the next room and able to return anytime I wanted.

Weeks later Diana sat in her home with Vincenzo and opened the box of my possessions I had on at the time of the wreck. In my topcoat she found a letter addressed to her.

"Dear Diana,

I look forward to our meeting with great anticipation. You see, this time when I leave Porter Ranch I'm leaving there for good. Your touch, your smell, your taste has been on my mind since I last saw you, and the thought of you makes me feel like we're kids again. I constantly reminisce about walking the streets of that small steel town we grew up in and first met. You are the all attaining mirage

in the desert, the dancing Northern Lights in my brain and the dream I want fulfilled. I regret the years we were apart my hometown girl, but I want to spend my remaining days with you. I love you Diana and I always will.
Pasquale"

She wept.....they both wept!